RISING FIRES

THE FIRE WITCH CHRONICLES 3

R.A. LINDO

PERIUM PUBLISHING

CONTENTS

AUTHOR'S NOTE

The Fire Witch Chronicles is a spin-off series, following a character from the **Kaira Renn Series.**

There's no need to read the Kaira Renn Series, but please be aware there are some references to the original series.

WELCOME TO A MAGICAL UNIVERSE

Welcome to the secret, magical universe of **The S.P.M.A. (The Society for the Preservation of Magical Artefacts.)**

As my readership grows, it's nice to have a way of staying in regular contact. My **mailing list** is one way. You'll only hear from me when I've got exclusive previews or new releases.

You can join **my private Facebook group** where all things S.P.M.A. are discussed.

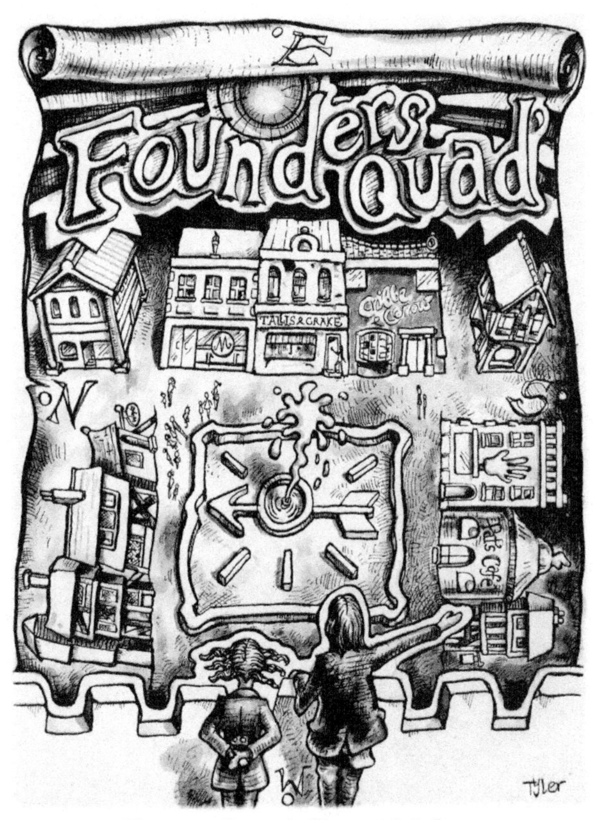

Founders' Quad Map

Society Square Map

1

MORNING GATHERING

The top floor of Zucklewick's is as homely as I remember — a log fire keeping us warm as we ponder the changing tide in the skies. Zucklewick's is the Society bookshop situated in Founders' Quad, catering for the above-ground world and the magical one — a particular charm revealing magical secrets hidden within ordinary looking books.

The four of us have met on the top floor to go over recent events, including Kaira's return and how it links to the mysteries in the sky. There's also the question of Taeia's training, Casper hoping that attaching the lost boy to Jacob will tame the darkness in him. It won't be long before Taeia reaches the official wizarding age of eighteen when he'll be able to travel wherever he pleases, including to the sky realms.

His use of a charm laced with a curse means his penchant stone has dimmed: a sign he's close to being shut out from the magical travel gifted to Society members. The only reason he can still access Periums is because the

S.P.M.A. allows certain charms laced with dark magic: one of the changes after the last war.

We learnt the hard way that ignoring Gorrah (dark magic) has its downsides, particularly when you're dodging curses on the battlefield. Now, it's a case of delicate engagement, including the Domitus' use of a mild curse in their taming of the Silverbacks. Pure Gorrah ends your days in the S.P.M.A. so Taeia's lucky to still be here.

He's currently getting a taste of grand wizardry from the uncle who's agreed to train him, more for self-preservation than anything else. With the bad news sinking in that Taeia's the heir to The Winter King, certain plans have been put in motion, including keeping a close watch over his behaviour in The Cendryll: his new home after Jacob came to his rescue on The Hallowed Lawn.

Facing down a furious, white Williynx is no one's idea of fun, and the only reason Taeia's still alive is the compassion the Renns are famous for. I just hope he finds that same quality in himself before it's too late, or we'll have another battle on our hands.

Our Night Ranging continues, allowing me to discover new realms whilst keeping an eye on familiar ones. There's something *magnetic* about mysteries surrounding the S.P.M.A., though, the new one lying in the fragile triangle of allegiance in the stars. Our morning meeting in Zucklewick's was Conrad's idea, helping Lucy and Noah come to terms with a sudden change to our Night Ranging routine.

They're annoyed they can't travel to the sky realms until they've received more advanced training, arguing they're as equipped as we are for battle. It takes patience and a lot of persuasion to convince them otherwise. Kaira's suggested the need for more training and since she's the only one of us who's travelled to the sky realms, it makes sense to listen to her.

Lucy and Noah are brilliant Night Ranger companions but they haven't faced fierce battle, something certain Society elders will prepare them for. Hopefully, it won't come to that but we need to prepare for all eventualities.

Farraday's busy dealing with Taeia's old crew who are also staying in The Cendryll, awaiting a decision about their futures. It's fair to say that Fillian, Mae and Alice's Night Ranging days are over, although whether that means a return to the above-ground world is yet to be seen.

CONRAD AND I ARE SITTING NEAR THE FIRE, OFFERING ALL THE details we've got about Kaira's visit and where this is likely to lead us. Noah and Lucy sit in the armchairs on either side of the coffee table. It's where Ivo Zucklewick comes to relax when he gets the chance, the bookshop having a direct link to the Society library known as The Pancithon. Ivo's a night owl so is usually found roaming the Pancithon at night.

I listen to Ivo below, opening up Zucklewick's to the keen shoppers waiting outside. Founders' Quad comes alive soon afterwards — another busy day for the members who run the above ground establishments. Along with keeping a pristine bookshop, Ivo is also a master of subtle magic, suggesting a Blindman's Watch might come in handy with Taeia's arrival in The Cendryll.

A Blindman's Watch is a pamphlet acting as a surveillance device. You tuck it into a book near the location of the person you're tracking, opening the pamphlet up to reveal all. Jacob's got a plan to carry a book on him from now on, leaving it in the classroom he's using for his lessons.

As long as Taeia remains under suspicion, all necessary precautions need to be taken.

"So, we stick to Night Ranging while you have fun in the sky realms?" Noah queries, playing with the buttons on his waistcoat.

He's clearly not pleased that he and Lucy have been side lined temporarily, although I remind him again that it's Kaira's orders.

"We won't be going anywhere until Kaira returns," I explain, putting another log on the fire. "The Night Ranging continues as normal until we've got a clear path to the skies."

"To The Winter King," Lucy adds, looking like she's taken the news better than Noah.

"Right."

"And how long's our training going to take?" Noah prompts.

"Until the Society elders are happy you're equipped for whatever's ahead of us," Conrad replies, sitting cross legged alongside me. "Hopefully, it's more of an adventure than anything else, but meeting Sianna Follygrin and Aarav Khan weren't coincidences: the two people likely to prepare us for the skies. Whatever's going on up there is likely to involve a degree of danger."

"Danger we should be walking into?" Noah challenges.

"Danger we choose to walk into," I reply as the fire crackles. "Night Ranging's our official role; the sky realms are a choice. If it means helping a Winter King in need, meaning things staying calm in the skies and down here, I'm in."

"When do you think Kaira will be back?" Lucy asks, holding out her arms to feel the warmth of the fire.

"Soon," I say, feeling a familiar rhythm building with an

old friend. "Until then, we help Jacob during the day and keep an eye on things at night."

"I'm not sure I'm ready to step onto a battlefield?" Lucy adds, her right foot tapping nervously. "Monitoring malevs is one thing, but going to battle with Bloodseekers ... I don't know if I'm cut out for that."

"Only one way to find out," Noah replies, offering Lucy a reassuring smile. "Return to Zilom and The Royisin Heights to learn from the best. My uncle rubs me up the wrong way but there's no doubting his magical abilities. He's a sky soldier, after all, perfectly placed to prepare us."

"And Sianna will hopefully tell us more about her unofficial role," Conrad adds. "Looks like she hasn't hung up her wand yet."

"We've got time to make up our minds before Kaira returns," I add, heading over to the window to study Founders' Quad. "Whether to stay here or travel to the skies."

I look down on the busy streets, my mind already made up. When Kaira returns, I'll head to the sky realms with her, ready to meet a fading Winter King and the Bloodseekers closing in on his white fortress. As the streets of Founders' Quad begin to fill, I think about the incredible journey I've been on ... from magical sweets to menacing Melackin and a battle to the death in shifting sands.

New adventures are on the horizon now, hovering in a magical universe hidden in the stars: a brooding world of wonder about to reveal its mysteries. Conrad appears alongside me, offering me a smile. He's come round to the idea of defending comrades not directly linked to us, remembering those who came to our aid: sky urchins, ageing giants and Society legends risking their lives to protect ours.

The tables are turned now, the youngest wizards flying

to the aid of a fading few: beauty and unity at the heart of everything we do.

"Ready to travel to the unknown again?" Conrad asks as he stands alongside me.

He's dressed in jeans and a white T-shirt, the scar running along his neck a mark of his bravery and sacrifice. My scars are lighter, marking my arms and legs and I'm sure I'll acquire more soon enough.

"It's what we do best," I reply, studying Conrad's green eyes that lack the concern they previously had. "We've got pretty good at navigating our way through trouble."

"It was nice to have some peace and quiet for a while, allowing us to have some fun in the skies."

"We can still have some fun," I say, stepping closer to my boy wizard, "we just might have to dodge a few Bloodseekers along the way."

"Sounds like paradise," Conrad jokes, his smile signalling he's committed to the journey ahead.

"I say we fly to Zilom," I say to Lucy and Noah, stepping away from the window. "Get up to speed with things happening in the sky realms. By the sound of things, Aarav's going to be our guide, preparing us for whatever's needed."

"Then onto The Royisin Heights," Noah adds. "The setup of Sianna's dwelling allows her to see the sky, meaning she's the best person to help us read the stars. I don't know why that's going to matter but I think it will."

"Maybe the stars work like a Nivrium," Lucy suggests, getting up from the armchair to stand by the fire. "A Nivrium allows us to read water, helping us to judge the temperature of the Society. The stars marking the sky realms could do the same, assuming we can learn how to read them: flickering in certain patterns to show stability and danger."

"Brilliant, Lucy," Noah adds, running a hand through his long, dark hair.

"Brilliant indeed," I echo, wondering if Lucy's about to discover a lot more than battle charms in our new adventures.

"So, Zilom then The Royisin Heights," Conrad echoes. "Gather the information we need before Kaira returns."

We all nod in agreement before Noah adds, "Is there any food up here?"

"I doubt Ivo would thank us for raiding his cupboards," I reply, "but Jacob makes a mean cooked breakfast."

"Hasn't he got to teach?"

"It's still early and he'll want to know our plan anyway. Come on, let's use Ivo's Scribberal to send Jacob a message, then back to The Cendryll for some breakfast."

"What's it like?" Lucy asks as we prepare to leave via the door near the fire. "Battle, I mean."

"Like a brutal orchestra playing a perfect harmony," I reply, surprising myself with the response. "It's unforgettable and unforgivable at the same time, but we've got legends on our side and a unity that's hard to shatter. Don't worry, Lucy — if we run into battle you'll be ready."

"Well, I can't wait to meet some Bloodseekers," Noah offers with a smile, ducking as Lucy swipes at him.

They're a cute couple, finding their way in the romantic way of things as our magical universe revolves around us, preparing to send us spinning towards the stars.

2

FAMILIAR REALMS

With breakfast eaten and Jacob brought up to date with our plans, we take to the skies on the back of our trusted Williynx, heading to the land of suspended rain. Zilom's one of the more spectacular realms in the S.P.M.A., multiple strands of illuminated raindrops hanging in the air, acting as Periums for welcome visitors.

It always reminds me of standing inside the world's biggest chandelier when I'm on the ground, even more beautiful from the sky: a vision of swaying light illuminating the streets. The strand of light we're looking for is decorated in the combined colours of our penchant stones, but the morning light makes this more difficult to detect so we fly lower, making a point of waving to the witches and wizards going about their daily business.

The waves are a sign of reassurance that we're not following in the footsteps of Taeia's crew, now under strict supervision in The Cendryll. It's obvious a few Society members are still nervous at the sight of a group of young

Night Rangers in the sky, so I suggest sending feathers of welcome.

"A shower of feathers to signal we're on a peaceful mission," I explain, patting my powder-blue Williynx in preparation.

"What if the feathers mess with the suspended rain?" Noah asks, remembering how our Williynx feathers transformed the hard ground of The Royisin Heights into a portal to the underground hideout.

"Good point," Lucy adds. "The last thing we want to do is offend anyone, particularly considering recent events here."

"Okay, a single feather from each of our Williynx," I contend. "A symbol of the beauty and unity we all live by."

"Can't do any harm," Conrad states, ruffling Erivan's turquoise feathers as he whispers the request.

Moments later, four feathers float down towards the streets where movement comes in waves, witches and wizards appearing from portal Periums before being transported onwards by a light beam of welcome. I flinch as my feather makes contact with the glittering raindrops closest to us, careful to hover above the suspended rain until we spot our strand of light calling us on.

Nothing disastrous happens but something beautiful does ... the sight of the four feathers connecting to the strand of light in question ... transforming it into a fountain of multi-coloured rain rising high into the sky.

"It's heading towards us," Conrad comments, tapping his ankles against Erivan to rise higher into the sky.

"Stay put," I say, realising that the use of the feathers has added a decorative element to our mode of transport this morning. "The fountain of rain is our way in."

"How do you know that?" Lucy asks, choosing caution over chance as she rises higher alongside Conrad.

"Guppy's right," Noah adds as the fountain of multi-coloured rain spins towards us like a tornado. "Williynx feathers only ever do good so there's nothing to worry about. If we pull away, it could be read as us declining the offer of welcome."

"You first," Lucy encourages with a smile.

Noah doesn't hesitate, resting lower on his fire-red Williynx before flying into the tornado of rain. I follow, holding on tight as Laieya — my powder-blue companion — spins towards the light show in the sky, submerging me into the heart of the fountain.

A blizzard of sound and colour surrounds me now, the endless spinning bringing on a bout of dizziness until the fountain reverts to strands of suspended rain, revealing a circle of light that Laieya touches down on.

Conrad and Lucy appear soon afterwards, covered in the same colourful glitter I am: a reminder of the magic that touches every part of the universe I call home. The circle of white light shines more intensely when our feet move closer to the boundary, reminding me of the Infernisi charm: a circle of light transforming into fire when the enemy tries to step beyond it.

I half expect the circle to vanish, sending us free falling into another new magical space but, instead, it stretches upwards ... reaching into the morning sky ... a potential portal to a world in the stars not yet open to us.

With our Williynx reduced to smaller forms, at ease within the shifting light of Zilom, I glance at the others before turning my attention to the silent sky above. Kaira's up there somewhere, negotiating a clear path for us. 'Shooting stars and twisted light' was how Kaira described access to the sky realms. Well, we've got the shaft of light but no evening sky to rain stars onto us.

"It's bound to be my uncle," Noah says, referring to the expanding shaft of light heading our way. "Always over the top."

"Great wizards have a right to indulge themselves, I suppose," Lucy counters, inspecting the colourful glitter in Noah's hair.

"Let's just hope he's better at getting to the point than most other adults," I add, adjusting the belt on my black, leather trousers: standard uniform nowadays. "If Aarav is the sky soldier overseeing activity between Zilom and the sky realms, he should be able to explain who's who up there: the realms, conflicts, potential allies and deadly enemies."

"I'm fairly sure we can put the Bloodseekers in the 'deadly enemies' category," Noah comments.

"Although Thylas Renn drinks the blood of the dead too," Conrad challenges, "helping to extend his life, so maybe it's more complicated than it looks."

I take out a vial of Fillywiss to help with a bout of dizziness. Sipping the purple liquid, I hand it to Lucy who's also trying to regain her equilibrium.

"Maybe we should build something while we wait," I suggest, remembering the romantic swing Conrad and I created in the Zilom sky recently.

"Looks like Aarav's almost here," Lucy replies, pointing to movement in the channel of light stretching from us to the heavens.

It's spectacular all right ... watching a speck of movement float down through the maelstrom of colour, surrounded by the same swirls of glitter decorating my clothes. Noah's right — his uncle is dramatic but drama is what we're heading into, meaning it's probably a good thing we've got a diva for a teacher.

"Is he dressed in pink?" Conrad queries as the thin, dark-skinned figure approaches ... hands outstretched in a messiah-like pose.

"Wait until you see the gold suit," Noah adds. "It makes him look like a robot."

"He's more flamboyant than Weyen Lyell, and that's saying something," I state, smiling to myself as the grand wizard surrounded by glittering raindrops reaches us, the intense gaze falling onto me as he touches down.

"You'll travel to the skies sooner than expected," Aarav offers in introduction, keeping his gaze on me for some reason. "Kaira is with Thylas Renn now, locked away in his fortress and formulating plans."

"Plans for us to travel there?" Lucy asks.

"In part, but all strategy revolves around a troubled heir yet to decide which side he's on: dark or light. Casper and Jacob have a job on their hands, trying to contain Taeia's fury."

"Jacob's got a healing touch," I reply, relieved when Aarav turns his gaze onto Noah. "Something he can't explain ... the way he halted Oweyna in her tracks before she ripped Taeia's head off, for example. If anyone can calm Taeia, Jacob can."

"Well, let's hope your brother's gifts are enough to stabilise a tilting wizard. The stars suggest otherwise although that doesn't help us in the present."

"So, you *can* read the stars," Noah comments, rubbing the glittering raindrops out of his hair.

"All sky soldiers can read the stars, Noah; it's a critical ritual required to track the movements of malevs seeking exile: Alice Aradel, for example. Alice made the mistake of showing her face in The Shallows, hoping her desperate bargain with Joseph Flint would buy her passage to the skies: the pirate economy of Kelph offering safe passage at a high price."

"Lucy thinks that stars forming the sky realms might work like a Nivrium," I add, nudging Lucy to explain more.

"It just makes sense that if reading the stars is important, it must act as a map ... a way of assessing the balance in the sky realms ... a bit like a Nivrium reading the temperature of the Society when it's filled with water."

"The very thing you're going to learn from Sianna soon enough," Aarav replies as he adjusts the lapel of his pink suit. "This morning is about increasing your understanding of the architecture of the sky: how it can be built, transformed and destroyed. It's the reason Farraday and Kerevenn arranged your previous visit here: the start of your familiarisation with a magical world in mid-air.

Once you've learnt to navigate an ever-changing world without the security of your Williynx, we will move on to the additional training Lucy and Noah require: the point at which Kaira will return to begin the first phase of travel. Thylas Renn is weak but remains a visionary. What he sees will determine our strategy in either containing or defeating Taeia when he discovers his destiny.

One more thing ... the raindrops covering your body act as your protection once you leave the ground ... brushing them off removes a safety net that comes in handy if the world you've built in the sky suddenly collapses around you. When the portal of light surrounding us returns to a white circle around our feet, step onto the edge of the circle and prepare yourself."

"For what?" Conrad asks.

"Flight without wings."

"You create the world of your choice in Zilom," Aarav begins as we step onto the edge of the circle.

Our Williynx choose to stay in the air, maybe because they're worried about us toppling out of the sky if things go wrong. It also makes me realise how much I still don't know about the S.P.M.A.

"Impermanence, however, is the source of the beauty here," Aarav continues. "Even the suspended rain transforms when required, as you discovered on your arrival. The issue with impermanence is its lack of stability, offering endless potential but obvious danger in battle. This circle is an example of this delicate balance."

I share a puzzled look with the others before the circle separates into four sections, lifting each of us into the air.

"I will dictate your path until you take control," Aarav continues, "precisely what will happen when you travel throughout the sky realms. Various energy fields will battle for your attention: loyal forces and shameless ones. It is *very* different to Periums where you dial in your location."

"So, it's more like using a Cympgus but without knowing your destination," I say.

"Precisely, Guppy, which limits your ability for imaginative control."

"So, how *do* we control where we're going?" Conrad asks, struggling to keep his balance on the single shard of light lifting us higher.

"Build a platform that stretches ahead in any direction until a vision of life appears."

"*Crystal clear,*" Noah comments sarcastically before almost losing his balance.

Lucy's already put the instructions into practice, imagining a bridge into life that she casually walks along. "Just think of somewhere we know like The Sinking Bridge."

Lucy has a particular attachment to The Sinking Bridge because it's where it all started with Noah — the 'Zoe thing' helping them to get closer. I decide on a steep ramp, stretching as far as the morning sky will allow, remembering a similar pathway that led me to my first meeting with the intense, mystical wizard guiding us now. Walking up the path is easier than it looks, gravity having little part to play in a realm of impermanent beauty.

"So, are you going to tell us what's going on *up there* ... beyond Thylas Renn needing our help?" Noah asks as we rise higher.

"Of course, Noah, but that will only become relevant if you choose to travel the skies. This is neither a given nor a recommended path to take, but as Society soldiers the choice is yours."

"So it *is* going to be dangerous?" Lucy prompts.

"Dangerous, mysterious and spectacular: a ride of a lifetime."

"Assuming we live to tell the tale," Conrad adds, reaching for my hand as we tilt suddenly.

"Life and death are givens, Conrad," Aarav replies, remaining poised in his pink suit and tie: a man reminding me more-and-more of Casper Renn each time I meet him. Kaira's dad hasn't got the peacock aspect to his personality, but they share the intensity and a rare wisdom — as if they've discovered a remedy that's developed a sixth sense for all things magical.

"How we choose to live life, however, is not. You and Guppy have tasted war and are forever marked by the experience. The question is, would you change it?"

"Nope," we both reply.

"Then you have your answer to the only question necessary: the same question my nephew and Lucy face now. When faced with danger, do we fight or fade ...? Courage is the elixir of life, after all, turning routine into revelation with each brave step."

"We're Night Rangers so we step in when necessary," Noah states, happy to get a reassuring nod from Lucy, "whether that's in The Society Sphere or up there."

"Count me in," Lucy echoes, smiling at the sight of the glittering raindrops swirling around her.

"Then it's time to learn about Devreack," Aarav states. "The realm of The Winter King."

With that, he utters an incantation to disintegrate the platforms we've built, watching as we reach out for the nearest strand of light, letting it slip through our hands as it senses our rhythm: a memory of our first descent through the Zilom skies.

As I gather hold of enough light strands to form a parachute, guiding me towards Noah's uncle, I get the feeling Aarav's style of training falls into the 'practical' category: a majestic wizard waiting to give us our first glimpse of a white fortress housing a fading king.

3

SKY DANCE

We end up standing on fine lines of light, reflecting our penchant stones' colour. It feels like I'm standing on a tightrope, struggling to keep my balance until I remember gravity's no threat here. The reassuring sight of Laieya resting on the line of light makes me feel better: a feathered friend for all seasons.

Standing high in the sky reminds me of the first time I walked under The Cendryll's skylight, heading towards Conrad and his dad who were hiding out for their own safety. Safety isn't a concern now I'm more familiar with the mysterious ways of Aarav, also pleased to see Noah relaxing in his uncle's presence.

Whatever issues Noah has with Aarav, he's fully aware of the situation we find ourselves in: a step up from tracking questionable witches and wizards in familiar realms. Tracking Bloodseekers and the like won't be as easy, mainly because there's another world waiting for us in the stars — one we're less familiar with, meaning mishaps are more likely.

Before we get to find out more about the uneasy allegiances in the sky realms, Aarav explains the incantation he used to destroy our platforms of light: a signal we're dealing with a lot of unknowns, including variations on the magical system that's become second nature to us.

"The difference between the sky realms and the earthly realms of the S.P.M.A. is their competing energies," Aarav explains, walking along his tightrope of light as if he's done this a million times. "Our Society has focused on peace for centuries, recently reminded of the need to balance dark and light as opposed to ignoring questionable sorcery. It is a balance we are proud to maintain, building a magical architecture which is grand in scale and surveillance."

"Sort of like a spectacular spying machine," Lucy comments before adding, "in a good way. There's always going to be someone who gets consumed by the magic we're blessed with, so we've got to have eyes everywhere."

Her yellow Williynx rests by her feet in miniature form, inspecting the tightrope of light intersecting with the others: a glimmering vision of a unified force.

"Yes, Lucy ... subtle surveillance as opposed to blunt interventions, but monitoring nevertheless. Peace and freedom are as fragile as they are rare: as are all forms of magic. After all, whatever can be built can be destroyed, including the most unique and powerful things."

"Like The Devenant," I add, remembering the shimmering beauty of the rainbow-coloured sky in Senreiya.

"Correct, Guppy," Aarav adds, glancing at me as I shift position on my tightrope of light.

Conrad has decided to sit on his seat in the sky, his legs swinging on either side of his blue ribbon of light. He gestures for me to do the same as Erivan — his turquoise Williynx — hovers in the air above him. I decide to stay put, keeping my focus on a man about to teach us new mysteries.

"Can you show us how to destroy platforms of light," I ask. "I've tried the Disineris charm but got nothing."

Turning to face me, Aarav whispers something indecipherable, sending me into a sudden free fall as my ribbon of light vanishes and the fun begins. With my Night Ranger crew grasping enough strands of light to control their direction of flight, I decide to do something else.

We're here to learn after all, already knowing how to create a parachute from the suspended rain. The first lesson learnt is linked to the multi-coloured raindrops surrounding our bodies, acting as a protective blanket when in mid-air: a safety net I'm about to put to the test.

"Guppy! Grab on!" comes the sound of Conrad's voice, but I've got a plan to accelerate this morning's lesson, whipping out my arm to send the protective blanket of rain swirling at speed ... a mini tornado of colour that reverses my free fall ... propelling me up towards the static figure of Aarav Khan who's decided to turn his protective shell of light into an umbrella. He's different, all right.

"What are you doing?" Conrad queries as I surge past him, ready to pirouette with a Society legend who's certainly dressed for the occasion: pink suit and multi-coloured umbrella at the ready. There's no incantation ... no magical word that makes the light platforms of Zilom vanish ... it's all imagined. I worked this out when Aarav made my platform disappear.

He didn't *say* anything, pretending to mouth a word to make us think otherwise. It's all part of the training: limited explanations and quick reactions seeming to be the style of the wizard in pink. With Conrad, Lucy and Noah looking on, held up by their parachutes of light, I put my theory to the test again, smiling as the ribbon of light vanishes beneath Aarav's feet.

He's prepared for this, of course, the reason he made an umbrella out of his protective layer of raindrops. It's the training we need to get to grips with the mysteries of Zilom and beyond ... my tornado of raindrops propelling me forward.

With Conrad, Lucy and Noah floating in mid-air, unsure whether they just study from a distance or join in, I utter 'Disira' to escape the suffocating rain, remembering Aarav's earlier point that 'you create the world of your choice' in Zilom.

I met him on a glittering precipice, looking down onto a past event: Taeia Renn attacking his own kind from the skies. Now, I need to meet him on my own terms, interpreting his words and movements as I vanish, re-appearing near my Night Ranger crew.

"Come on!" I shout to the others, watching as our Williynx have some fun of their own, maintaining reduced forms to dart through the strands of suspended rain. "Form a circle with me. It's about acting and reacting with limited charms."

Conrad gets what I mean, floating towards me. No Williynx and no defensive charms, just a focus on how we build and destroy light platforms in the sky — appearing, disappearing and re-appearing to avoid being trapped. Sianna's waiting to teach us more in The Royisin Heights, but first we need to learn the rules of travel: no Periums or penchants to protect us and no map of where we're headed.

"Is he always like this?" Lucy asks as the four of us move through the morning sky on platforms of light.

"Like I said, he's a diva," Noah replies, his blue cardigan covered with specks of multi-coloured rain. "Just telling us there's no spell to make light platforms would've been easier, but my uncle likes to do things his own way."

"What's he going to do now? And what's with the umbrella?"

"He always teaches with an umbrella," Noah replies, raising his eyebrows.

"I didn't know he taught."

"Only a few people, including me which I've tried to forget."

"Why?" I ask.

"Because it was pretty brutal. My uncle's old school so get ready."

Understanding the reason for Noah's resentment, we agree to navigate closer to Aarav, already thinking a few steps ahead. It isn't a battle of any kind, but it shares the same principles of action and intuition. You need to know your next position before you move there, adapting when it's obliterated or occupied until you find the rhythm of engagement. Our mystical teacher's giving no clues to the rhythm he's about to form, holding his umbrella above his head.

It's the umbrella that starts things, folding suddenly as it fires out a strand of white light that separates into sparks, stretching towards our spinning platforms. I'm gone before they reach me, remembering the Bildin charm is the secret to the Zilom skies: the spell that builds in seconds and fades just as quickly.

The white sparks of light follow our every move, forcing us into new positions — nothing dangerous like the creatures released from a Zombul, but we're not here to learn to defend ourselves; we're here to understand how magical travel is different in the sky realms.

Brooding and elegant, Aarav orchestrates things from mid-air. "Up there, you will battle with *energy* before any enemies make your acquaintance," he explains. "The sparks of light I've released represent the competing energy fields, showering down whenever you travel to the sky realms. They exist to test and tempt, drawing you towards each one until you make your choice. To get to your desired destination, first you need to learn how to *resist.*"

"Have you travelled there a lot?" Lucy asks.

"I live between worlds — the sky towers of Zilom sending me upwards when necessary. Now is one of those times."

"So, let's get on with the training so we can join you there," Conrad prompts, deciding to create an umbrella of his own, opening it to deflect the white sparks of light.

I find my own rhythm, stretching my protective blanket of glittering rain into a flying carpet for the fun of it. Noah sticks with tightropes of light, looking like a master weaver as he darts from one to another, staying in range to hear further instructions.

It's fun for now but I haven't felt the magnetic pull of a force field yet, something that intensifies with another blast from Aarav's umbrella — other colours added to a flood of energy, competing for our attention.

"Now, we get to the final part of this morning's test — the ability to resist the force of each energy field I've released. The white strands of light I originally sent out are your guiding light, representing the destination of choice. Your job is to continue to follow these strands as it becomes a path ... as high as you can go without being drawn off track."

"How will we know if we're getting it right?" I ask.

"You'll be able to stay on course, following the white channel of light until I end the lesson."

"And if we get it wrong?"

"A competing energy field will immerse you: the very

thing to be avoided when the real journey begins. It's time to test your resolve."

Our movements become more difficult as competing energy fields close in, literally taking my breath away as I struggle to stay near the path of choice. It's a *lot* harder than it looks, realising the Disira charm doesn't help when trying to escape the clutches of unwanted energy fields ... magnetic forces that begin to suffocate us as we try to surge on, keeping the pathway of pure light in our sights.

With the spiralling light racing upwards at speed, we move as one, using our different modes of travel to connect with it before a sudden temperature change slows our momentum ... the suffocating energy fields retracting when we do. What happens next is as stunning as it is surprising ... the sight of movement in the sky ... not of people or places but stars aligning ... forming a glittering map of a hidden wonderland.

"It's beautiful," I whisper as we edge closer, watching as interconnected triangles form, offering a portal to the *elsewhere*: a portal we're *definitely* not ready to travel through.

"What do we do now?" Lucy asks.

"Abandon flight," Conrad replies, uttering 'Propellus Celiri' before pulling on the flower stem that wraps itself around his wrist. "The Disira charm won't help us in unknown territory, so we drop as fast as we can."

"And if we suffocate in a competing energy field?" Noah asks, following Conrad's lead as he activates the flight charm.

"We won't get a chance to meet a Winter King."

"I get what you mean about brutal," I say to Noah, my white daisy spinning in a propellor motion, countering the trajectory of our spinning spiral of light. "Your uncle's training methods, I mean. It's like he's leaving us to sink or swim up here."

"He thinks fear should be part of all wizarding training," Noah replies, kicking his legs to accelerate his descent.

"Well, if a bit of adrenaline helps us to learn faster, I like it," Conrad comments.

As we successfully negotiate our way to safety, Aarav lowers his umbrella, turning the handle in his hand as if he's assessing our progress.

"You didn't look very concerned when we started to struggle," I say. "It's almost impossible to breathe when the competing energy fields close in."

"You're an advanced witch, Guppy, with experience in the field: you'll master sky travel soon enough. View this morning's lesson as a taste of things to come, including negotiating a Bloodseeker attack but that's for another day. Now it's time to learn more about the sky realms and the power hidden within Taeia Renn."

"TAEIA'S GOT HIDDEN POWER?" I ASK, SETTLING ON A STEEP ridge of blue light the four of us sit on.

"Yes, far more power than he realises," Aarav replies, standing in between the four of us. "His confused sense of allegiance diminishes his power, but it will be unleashed when he makes his choice."

"As in what side he's on?"

"Yes, so let's hope he chooses light over dark."

"What are the odds of that?"

"Slim. Although we won the battle to protect The Devenant, the ramifications of battle *up there* could rain down on us, presenting us with new problems."

"People heading this way, looking for shelter in the S.P.M.A.," Conrad adds, understanding the reason for the Society elders' concern.

"Indeed, Conrad. Survival will become the dominant instinct if the transition of power isn't smooth, which hopefully helps you to see the delicate situation we find ourselves in. Thylas and Taeia stand on opposing trajectories: one's power slipping away as the other is just discovering theirs. The realms surrounding Devreack already sense an opportunity, closing in on the white fortress protected by Williynx of the same colour, and a loyal army within.

Every drop of life leaving Thylas' body will echo within Taeia, until the internal conflict that troubles him so much becomes apparent ... his need to leave the S.P.M.A. but on his terms ... moving from the margins to the very centre of things with a dedicated following awaiting his arrival."

"So, Taeia will inherit Thylas' army of soldiers and white Williynx?" Lucy asks, swinging her legs over the steep ridge of light decorating the Zilom sky.

"Or an alternative army should he choose a different path."

"Hold on," Noah says with a puzzled look. "How can he choose a different path if he's the next Winter King?"

"By refusing to inherit the title," Conrad replies, "deciding on fury over unity. That's what happened to Erent Koll and all the other dark wizards with supreme powers: they use it to consume."

"You think Taeia could go as bad as Erent Koll?"

"Maybe. We don't really know him beyond his arrogant energy and taste for trouble. He might turn out to be the bully we think he is, or worse."

"What's Casper's plan?" I ask Aarav, keen for us to stay on the topic of strategy. Learning new incantations won't be much use if we're not navigating a clear path to an end game: the peaceful transition of power from one Winter King to another.

"To understand every aspect of Taeia's personality, specifically his psychological make up; this will give us some insight into the choice he's likely to take."

"The reason Jacob's using a Blindman's Watch to keep a track of Taeia," I add, realising that every event leading to this point is linked, including Joseph Flint's trips to The Shallows to meet Alice Aradel. The evening witch was trying to buy safe passage to the sky realms until we intervened.

Then there was the Domitus who tried to attack us in Drandok, flying on tamed Silverbacks at night, hoping to read the secrets in the stars. Sianna Follygrin offered us help in The Royisin Heights soon after our meeting in Zilom.

With the sky realms tempting malevs in hiding, I can see the potential scale of the problem — the possibility of powerful sky forces offering sanctuary to exiled S.P.M.A. members, until we've got a storm of resentment ready to rain down on us ... the vision of Bloodseekers swarming dead bodies occupying my mind. All it takes is one bad wizard to disrupt everything, and this time it's a Renn.

My money's on Taeia being a nightmare Winter King, his ego growing by the second once he realises the power hidden within him, breaking the chain of legendary Renns giving their lives to protect the S.P.M.A. The thought makes me thirsty all of a sudden, something easily sorted by a trip to The Singing Quarter later.

Our dapper teacher hasn't got singing in mind, opening his umbrella to release another shower of glittering light ... not to suffocate or test us but, instead, to show us what we've all been waiting to see ... the interconnected lands in the sky

... stretching and contracting as if they rest uneasily with one another.

"Get comfortable because this may take some time," Aarav explains, spinning the umbrella to add a different colour to each space in a shimmering representation of the sky realms, making me wonder how soon we'll return to a battlefield of a different kind.

4

TESTING TIMES

We're not looking at the interconnected stars forming the sky realms, but a much smaller version of it created by Aarav's use of the Canvia charm. Typically used to draw or write things out of necessity or boredom, it's the perfect spell to show us the magical world hidden in the stars.

As I sit alongside Conrad on the blue ridge of light, Noah taps me on the shoulder as the triangle floating in the Zilom sky rotates slowly, revealing realms decorated by names: Whistluss, Zordeya and Neferell.

Our Williynx hover around the glimmering triangles, tapping at the edges with their beaks as if they're inspecting a new addition to their world. We've been told the name of The Winter King's realm — Devreack — along with the pirate economy of Kelph, although some of the places within the rotating triangle remain blank. I lean forward, careful not to topple off our platform in the sky.

"Get ready for a lecture," Noah whispers.

"Do you know the name of the other realms?" I ask Noah as Aarav adds the finishing touches to his design, twisting the umbrella of light as if he's painting a masterpiece.

"Nope. I'm as blind as everyone else."

"He's got an interesting way of teaching," Lucy adds, swinging her legs over the blue ridge of light.

"If you can call it that," Noah replies, still bitter about his early lessons in the company of his uncle.

I wonder how brutal the training was, knowing Noah can be a bit *dramatic*. So far, I've been impressed with Aarav: he's stylish, calm and gifted which has got my attention. The morning's moving on, though, and we need to fit in a trip to The Royisin Heights for our second lesson of the day.

"Where do you think the Bloodseekers hang out?" Conrad whispers as Aarav pivots on the ridge of light, placing the umbrella of light into his waistcoat pocket as if he's holstering a gun. It's a comedy moment I appreciate — the closest thing to a smile touching his face.

"Got to be Kelph," I reply to Conrad's question, feeling his hand on my lower back.

We're going to be lost in Society business soon, so maybe his touch is a reminder not to lose sight of each other when we do. Either way, it's a simple touch of love I appreciate as our education continues.

"You may notice that Devreack is the pinnacle of the triangle," Aarav begins, deciding to elongate the ridge of blue light, allowing us to get closer to the glittering creation. "This is because the realm of The Winter King is the original sky realm."

"So, there was only one?" Conrad asks.

"In the beginning, yes," our stylish guide replies, gesturing for us to stand and join him as the ridge of light stretches out under his feet, placing him inches away from the rotating triangle of light.

"Like our ancient universe, the sky realms have expanded over the centuries, leading to a magnificent world of wonder. The neighbouring realms of Devreack — Whistluss and Zordeya — have remained loyal to The Winter King; this is unlikely to change with the impending arrival of Taeia Renn."

"Because he's a nutter," Noah comments as the four of us study the map of light.

"Because he's unstable, Noah, but we will reserve judgement until we're sure of his intentions."

"Well, he's firing down at his own people," Noah challenges, looking as if he wants to start an argument.

"And you've made similar mistakes in your time here, so I would advise caution in judgment. We all know of wizards deemed to be dark who have turned out to be our saviours."

"Isiah Renn," I comment, remembering the terrible sacrifice Kaira's grandfather made to save her — one of the reasons Kaira kept her distance for so long, maybe.

"Yes ... Isiah, Guppy. A legend and fallen hero who is remembered on The Hallowed Lawn: a place of rest few would have imagined for him not so long ago. Isiah taught us many things, including the subtle distinction between a malev and a master of magic."

"A master needs to be able to negotiate all forms of magic," Conrad adds, remembering how suspicious everyone was of Isiah — until he absorbed a book of evil to work out the weakness in a lethal artefact.

I can still see it now ... black bile spilling out of him as Casper's face changed, realising his dad had been right all along. Isiah's point was simple: if you ignore dark forces, you give them the upper hand. We learned *that* lesson the hard way.

"Correct, Conrad," Aarav replies, pointing at the name

Kelph in a narrow section of the triangle. "These people will attempt to draw Taeia into their world: a grand, brutal tribe with a taste for power."

"Perfect for Taeia, then," Lucy comments, reaching out to touch the dots of light swarming around the realm signalling danger. "What are they?" she asks in reference to the swarming dots.

"Bloodseekers. A feral group with no allegiance, happy to offer their services to the highest bidder."

"Which is why they hang around Kelph?"

"Yes, because loyalty has little place amongst pirates. The principle of piracy, after all, is to steal, and they've long sought the greatest prize."

"The throne of The Winter King," Noah adds, parking his resentment to focus on the job at hand.

I watch as Noah takes a step closer to his uncle — the first step towards a truce between them, maybe. Noah hasn't worked this out yet, but he's got something in common with Taeia: a bitterness towards an uncle who's kept his distance. Unlike Taeia, this resentment hasn't morphed into mad attacks on his comrades but I'm surprised he doesn't see the root of the conflict in the boy destined to be king: a wizard living in the shadow of a Society legend who's done his best to keep his distance.

"A throne we must protect at all costs," Aarav replies, placing a hand on his nephew's shoulder, "and the Society elders have faith in each of you: Night Rangers gifted in the art of flight and mediation. Mediation is *key* to our travel, avoiding conflict wherever possible."

"When do you think Kaira will be back?" I ask as Lucy moves towards Conrad and me, giving Noah and his uncle some space.

"Soon after your meeting with Sianna. When you can

read the stars, you will make your first quest. Thylas is keen to meet you all, impressed with your exploits at such a young age."

"What's he like?" Lucy asks, watching a vision of the sky realms fade in the morning sky.

"Everything you would expect a king to be: regal, powerful and wise. Time catches us all, however, and Thylas doesn't have much time left. Your job is to meet his allies and know his enemies, which is when the true journey begins."

THE WINTER QUARTER IS QUIET THIS MORNING, A SMALL gathering of witches and wizards walking through the snow-covered streets. The perpetual snow is always a wonder to see, particularly when you're gliding through it and looking down on a winter wonderland. The snow only falls in the hidden, magical part, leaving the above-ground world to make do with a faint light decorating ramshackle buildings.

We decided on The Chattering Tap before we left Aarav in Zilom, thanking him for our introduction to a new form of sky travel and our first glimpse of the hidden wonders in the stars. We were close to getting a *real look* during our training session, battling with suffocating light.

When the time comes, we'll be ready for Bloodseekers and the pirate army in Kelph, but for now I need a sip of a particular remedy, looking forward to watching magical traffic pass the windows of The Chattering Tap. We enter and sit at my favourite table closest to the door. A few regulars occupy the bar, including Joseph Flint who offers an awkward smile when he sees us.

I still feel a little bad about intervening on Joseph's little party with Alice Aradel, but at least he didn't get into trouble for it — plus Alice coming out of hiding was the trigger for everything, trying to make a dark bargain with the shady lot in Kelph, hoping to gain access to the sky realm attracting Bloodseekers and the like.

Luckily, Conrad and I got to the evening witch in time, putting a stop to her plan and sending her on her way to The Velynx: a fair trade for trying to kidnap us a few years ago. Lorena Lellant does her usual flirting when she takes our order, focusing on Conrad and ignoring the rest of us.

"Four Liqins, please."

"Sure, gorgeous," comes the reply Conrad does his best to ignore.

If I was the jealous type, I'd whisper a charm to shut her up, but it gets less annoying each time she does it, especially as Conrad barely seems to notice her.

"Well, we've got a better idea of the geography of the sky realms," Lucy says as we wait for a sweet remedy to arrive — one that helps with disorientation and hysteria.

None of us seem particularly affected by this morning's lesson, even Noah who seems to have made some progress with his uncle. We gave them the distance they needed, re-joining our Williynx for a bit of fun in the suspended rain. Whether it's helped heal old wounds is anyone's guess, but the signs were promising.

"Your uncle's a pretty good teacher," I say to Noah, watching a group of wizards appear on the snow-covered streets outside. "I like the way he spun us towards the sky realms, making us feel out of our depth before landing us safely on the ridge of light: intense but good."

"He was the same when he trained me," Noah comments, unbuttoning his waistcoat and pulling on the neck of his black T-shirt. "I always thought it was about humiliation, but now I know it wasn't."

"He doesn't seem like a cruel man," Lucy adds, placing a hand on Noah's arm: a reassuring touch to calm his agitated state.

"Farraday was the same," I say. "He used a Zombul to release a Viadek on us: a massive, fire-spitting monster that completely threw me. Jacob went mad until Farraday explained all creatures released from a Zombul are under the user's control — not the case in a real battle. It was his way of waking us up to the reality of war ... maybe what Aarav's doing for us now."

"I feel like an idiot," Noah says as he turns to look out of the window, his attention on the snow-globe shape of Velerin's: the restaurant he and Lucy are likely to go to soon. The Sinking Bridge comes after the meal, penchants placed on it, testing the intensity of a couple's love. "I've basically ignored my uncle every time I've seen him recently ... the reason he tends to vanish when I appear."

"Like he did on our first trip to Zilom," Conrad replies.

"Yep. Probably sick of my sarcastic comments."

"Go easy on yourself, Noah. You couldn't have known he was preparing you for something big."

"And there's me thinking *Night Ranging* was big."

"It *is*," Lucy challenges. "It helps to keep the S.P.M.A. at peace."

"Yep, sure, but I always thought my uncle had been cruel in training for the sake of it, throwing things at me I couldn't handle. Now I know why."

"Which is where forgiveness begins."

"Wise words, Lucy Flint. Where's this Liqin, anyway? I need about four of them before we head off again."

"To gaze at the stars," Conrad adds in a comical manner,

reaching out for Noah's hand who pretends to swing for him. "Come on," Conrad teases, helping to lift Noah out of his gloomy mood. "Best mates, studying the stars ... I'm getting all warm just thinking about it."

"You can keep your warmth to yourself," Noah jokes, happy to forget about his unappreciative attitude towards his uncle for a while.

"Well, here's to our new teacher," I say, raising my glass: a toast to a pink-suited wizard, offering a glimpse of what's to come.

5

CONTINUING LESSONS

The Royisin Heights sit in a familiar darkness, the large mounds of earth decorating the landscape a reminder of different ways of living in the S.P.M.A. I can't get my head around witches and wizards who *choose* to live outside of The Society Sphere but, then again, I'm only sixteen and have only scratched the surface of our magical universe.

We've arrived in the company of our feathered companions to seek out Sianna Follygrin — the woman who appeared on our first visit here, offering us shelter in her hideaway before giving us a glimpse of the labyrinth structure hidden below. Through Sianna's stained-glass floor, we peered through into the underground world of The Royisin Heights, full of disfigured Society members hiding out in a place lined with remedies.

Mixing certain remedies creates temporary disfigurement. Also, there are remedies that ease the pain of the permanently scarred, like Farraday. We bumped into Farraday here on the trail of Neve Blin: a Domitus in disguise who ran into trouble in Drandok. Like Alice Aradel, Neve retreated to this silent wilderness, finding a way underground where she could mask her identity.

It's hard to live on your wits when all you've got is favours to call in, and Alice and Neve quickly ran out of malevs and Melackin to do their bidding. The Velynx is taking care of them now — the blistered faculty housing bad things and bad people.

Speaking of bad people, I've got Bloodseekers on my mind for some reason, keen to use my Follygrin to find out what they look like. No doubt they'll be tracking us down as soon as we enter the sky realms, and I want to be ready for all eventualities.

The wind lifts as we touch down, patting our Williynx in thanks as we try to locate Sianna's home, formed from the burgeoning earth. The Royisin Heights stretches *on* and *on*, covered in hundreds of mounds, so we rely on our Williynx to track Sianna's scent. I think of using their magical feathers for a second ... feathers that transform everything they touch ... but I doubt Sianna would thank me for this, likely to withdraw the help we're going to need.

The fact that Casper's asked Aarav and Sianna to help makes our actions even more important. As calm as Kaira's dad is, he's not a man to be messed with, particularly when duty calls: a duty to protect beyond our own magical realm.

I can never see myself wanting out and ending up in a place like this, but Sianna probably felt the same at my age, gradually losing the taste for all things magical as her grandfather succumbed to the demands of duty.

Sianna explained her retreat here as an escape from the same fate, never wanting to be bound by Society duty in the same way, which makes her role as a sky soldier a bit of a puzzle: a reclusive witch wanting a quiet life but ending up studying the stars.

Whatever her reasons, I'm pleased she's agreed to map the stars for us — a reminder of another Society hero who provided the critical piece to end the last war: her grandfather Francis Follygrin.

The Follygrins are energy readers, making them perfect comrades in troubled times. Now, it's just a case of following our Williynx who track the ground with their beaks, maintaining their majestic forms in the dark wilderness ... a striking vision of turquoise, powder-blue, red and yellow adding some well-needed colour to a lifeless realm.

"Here," Conrad says with a nudge, offering me a vial of Crilliun: magical eyedrops to help you see in the dark.

We've got our Quivvens stored in our Keepeasies, but these are only used when danger's a possibility. The only danger here is boredom, following our feathered friends as they inspect mound after mound, attempting to locate Sianna's.

"Why don't we just fly there?" Noah asks, taking the vial of Crilliun from me.

"I got the feeling our Williynx wanted us to land," Conrad replies, using his own stash of magical eyedrops to improve his vision.

"Me too," Lucy adds, kicking her feet into the soil as we walk through the vast wilderness. "Maybe Sianna wasn't impressed with our first visit here. You know, when we had a bit of fun."

"Our little light show," I add, remembering how we lit up the sky out of boredom, having no idea how to enter any of the private dwellings. "It didn't do any harm."

"You don't know that, Guppy," Conrad adds. "It might have annoyed the people that live here."

"They never leave their homes so why would it bother them?" Noah queries, blinking as the eyedrops work their magic.

"Precisely because they never leave their homes," Lucy replies. "They want to be left in peace, meaning no interruptions."

"I'd rather live above ground."

"Never," I counter. "Live *above ground* rather than here? What about the underground world beneath our feet? And the ability to fly away from here in seconds, taking us to a million magical places. We could be in Gilweean in minutes before heading to Senreiya, or back to The Cendryll and the hundred Periums transporting us somewhere new. You'd be *mad* to ever live above ground again."

"But they don't *do anything* here," Noah adds, using his arm to point out the obvious: no movement or life evident. "What's the difference between sitting in a mound of earth and sitting above ground watching TV? They're both pointless."

"You think the people here just sit inside?" Lucy asks.

"What else are they doing? Praying?"

"I thought we were going to lose the sarcasm."

"Okay, sorry," Noah offers. "I'm hungry and want to speed up whatever this is. Conrad and Guppy are off when Kaira gets back, and we've got to stay here, scrambling around various places to find new teachers."

"You don't have to travel with us," Conrad states as his turquoise Williynx lifts its head, squawking softly to signal we've arrived at Sianna's dwelling. "If all the plans and teaching's getting to you, just stick to Night Ranging. We won't be gone forever."

"You think I'm going to leave you on your own up there?" Noah replies with a smile, realising he's fallen into a gloomy mood again. "You're going to need your guardian angel with you."

"My guardian angel? I thought you were coming along to do the cooking."

Conrad and Noah share a smile and we turn our attention to the mound of earth. I watch the lines of soil run down the side, remembering how they formed around our feet, running up our bodies until it covered our penchants. As we're pulled towards the mound of earth, I wave goodbye to Laieya, leaving her to blast into the dark sky with her colourful companions, a single feather from each signalling their exit.

Sianna Follygrin is standing by the fireplace with her back to us, looking in the mirror as if it's a window into something else, which it probably is. She doesn't say anything for a while, leaving us to stand in her comfy home that looks out onto the sky. I look up at the sky as we wait, wondering where the invisible perimeter of her dwelling extends to. The lack of external sound suggests there is one, but maybe that's another trick at play.

If anyone's educated in the history of magic, it's going to be Sianna. After all, she's the granddaughter of a man who pretended to be dead for decades, creating complex security measures to stay hidden from prying eyes. Whenever I met her grandad Francis Follygrin, I felt honoured to be in his presence. Not because he made me feel that way, but more to do with how the adults behaved around him.

Casper and Philomeena took us with them when they visited, leading us through a water chamber, taking us through a maze of tunnels. The tunnels led to a room reached after a *long* walk up a steep hallway. It was like visiting an all-seeing wizard who only revealed what was necessary, holding critical answers to important questions.

In the end, it turned out Francis had the answer to the *most important* question, giving us the upper hand in a blood chamber of death.

"I imagine you're hungry," Sianna says as she turns to face us.

She's dressed in silver today, a loose-fitting dress that covers her feet. The powder on the floor lifts as she walks across it, making me think our lesson's already started.

"Starving," Noah replies, looking around for any food on offer. "A glass of Semphul will do," he adds, referring to the hunger remedy typically reserved for the battlefield.

"Semphul or a feast?"

I glance at Conrad and Lucy, wondering at the change in Sianna's personality. Our first visit here was stand offish, the offer of a warm remedy and some information. There was definitely no feast on offer which makes me wonder why the change in mood.

Maybe we were viewed as annoying kids then, barging in on reclusive witches and wizards who wanted to be left alone. Whatever the reason, I'm not going to turn down food because who knows how long this lesson's going to last.

"Feast!" we all say, sharing an awkward look when our host doesn't move.

"Well, you know the way."

The way refers to the six passageways leading off the room — the only one lit by candles the obvious choice. I take Conrad's hand as I gesture for Lucy and Noah to follow.

"Come on," I whisper, "before she changes her mind."

With our second lesson of the day on hold, I step into the illuminated passageway with Conrad, wondering what wonders lay in store for us.

6

A TASTE OF DANGER

The room we walk into doesn't have a stained-glass floor or fragments of glass buried in the walls, meaning we've walked into another mysterious alcove in the home of a reclusive witch. Although Sianna says she's turned her back on Society duty, she's clearly involved in some way and I can't help thinking of the similarities she shares with her grandad.

A frail, old man who lived his life hidden away in the maze-like structure deep within Follygrin's, Francis was the man who gave Kaira her Follygrin, and the one person Casper and Philomeena relied on to shed light on dark events. In the end, he became imprisoned in an obsessive guard over a lethal artefact: a fate he encouraged us to avoid.

My last memory of Francis is sitting in the middle of a stone cell, broken and fading as the Terrecet fragment was released from its cell in the ceiling, placed into the hands of the small Society army who eventually destroyed it. We haven't walked into any sort of cell, and there's nothing locking Sianna into a life in a magical wilderness, but she's clearly been unable to escape her granddad's sense of duty.

The promised feast fills the table dominating the room we enter — the biggest table I've ever seen that fills a space *way* bigger than it looks from the outside. Sianna still likes the touch of brilliance magic offers, the space above the table filled with multi-coloured ribbons of light.

I reach up for one of the ribbons, reminded of the glittering raindrops in Zilom, remembering how the sky towers oversee travel to and from the sky realms.

"Take a seat," Sianna says as I glance at the food on offer: pies, sandwiches, salads, fruits and *loads* of cakes.

Noah dives in, reaching for the high-backed chair closest to him, stopped in his tracks by a vision of blue perched on the end of the table — a bird I first saw in the fields of Senreiya: a Jacqus. They're the birds responsible for protecting the section of The Devenant housed in Senreiya, although I never saw how they did it, hoping we'll get a display of their unique powers before we've polished off the feast.

Whatever particular magic the Jacqus have, it's enough to make Noah think twice about attacking the food. For a boy who's always hungry, he's being surprisingly restrained.

"You're not going to let a little bird put you off, are you Noah?" Conrad teases as he sits alongside me, reaching for a handful of sandwiches as liquid pours from the swirls of light above us.

The liquid falls into the cups placed next to our plates, each remedy the colour of our penchant stone: a silent welcome from our reclusive host who watches us from one end of the table. It's weird to see someone standing so far away when you're eating, but I'm pretty sure things are about to get weirder so I pop a cake into my mouth, blinking as a fizzing sensation rushes through me.

"The cakes are injected with remedies from the underground section of The Royisin Heights," Sianna explains, placing her hand on the table for the Jacqus to perch on it. "Not the remedies you're used to."

"I feel like my head's going to explode," I comment, reaching for my blue remedy in the hope it eases the buzzing sensation: it doesn't.

"Are you all right, Guppy?" Conrad asks, deciding to leave the handful of sandwiches for a while.

My reddening face and neck suggests I'm not, which is the start of our second lesson of the day: the benefit of new remedies in a foreign land. With the four of us sat at one end of the table, suddenly not so keen to fill our stomachs with the feast on offer, Sianna sits down. Her silver dress glistens under the spiralling light above, the blue bird perched on her hand adding to the mystery.

The spirals of light lead to the sky ... no visible barrier separating Sianna's home and the wilderness beyond ... but there's no sound or movement at present ... only the sound of my chair dragging across the polished, wooden floor as I try to stand, feeling my legs give away.

"What sort of feast is this?" Conrad asks.

A flash of anger appears as he utters 'Promesiun' to generate a flood of protective light around his hands, which is when things *really* get interesting — the sight of a magnetic energy field reaching us in seconds.

The Jacqus spreads its wings, revealing a flurry of spectacular feathers but this is no peacock. A sudden blast of translucent, blue light creates a barrier between us and our increasingly weird host ... a barrier that stretches around us until I feel the full force of the Jacqus: a crushing sensation that makes me double over.

There's no sign of Sianna now and the table's also vanished, the blinding barrier separating the space we're in feeling like a no-man's-land of confusion. Why would a comrade prepare a feast of spiked food with a magical, blue bird acting as security? It's not the lesson I had in mind, holding onto the back of my chair to keep my balance.

With the remedies pouring down from the spinning circles of light above us, I feel Conrad helping me back to my chair followed by the sound of a muffled apology. Something weird's going on, all right, but if Casper Renn has planned these lessons there's more to this visit than a feast of slow poison.

"Do you mind telling us what's going on?" Lucy asks, turning to check on me as the barrier of blue light moves towards us — the silhouette of Sianna visible somewhere within it. I say *within* because space is different here, stretching and contracting like an optical illusion. Everywhere I look seems to shift position, forcing me to lower my head to avoid vomiting over the party food.

"A lesson in simple acts," Sianna replies, her voice echoing through the translucent barrier courtesy of a tiny, blue bird with the ability to flood any space with blinding light. I'm wondering what else the Jacqus can do as the blue wall of light pivots horizontally, hovering above the table. "First, trust nothing offered in the sky realms because you won't spot your enemies."

"Great," Noah replies with his usual sarcasm, reluctant to devour the food on offer.

"Are you going to *help* Guppy or just give us a lecture?" Conrad asks, wary of activating any other charms.

"The blue remedy will cure Guppy of a mild nausea," comes Sianna's reply from God knows where.

It looks like the wall of defensive light can morph and adapt at will, the strange weight of it pressing down on me as I reach for my cup of blue liquid, gulping it down in good faith.

"What's with the Berlin wall?" Noah asks, getting up from his chair as the light hovers lower, resting over the feast no-one's keen to tuck into.

"A symbol of what you can call on in times of need. There are other escape routes of course, like the Disira charm, but until you know your terrain, let the Jacqus map your route to safety."

"How do we call them?" I ask, feeling instantly better with the remedy tingling through me.

"The Exhibius charm," Sianna says, appearing through another of the tunnels to our left. "Of course, this will only work in critical situations; the Jacqus don't stand on duty like the Williynx."

It's interesting that Sianna mentions our feathered friends because they're nowhere to be seen at the moment: a sign of their complete trust in our host and the process she's taking us through.

"Is that it?" Noah asks, feeling annoyed our feast has been ruined by an over-dramatic display.

"No," Sianna replies, lifting her silver dress as the blue wall of light fades. "You need to wear your Quivvens at all times in the sky realms, providing you with protection of different kinds."

"Our Quivvens will help us to see when we're blind," Lucy comments, studying the remedies that continue to pour down from the ceiling — endless taps of liquid relief for a group of Night Rangers about to embark on a *very different* mission.

"Yes, Lucy, but not just on your travels and in battle. As I said, trust nothing you're offered up there; the Quivven will determine the properties of anything you consume."

"Like a Nivrium for the stomach," Noah quips, his stomach growling now as the feast looks tempting again. "Can we practice now? On the feast, I mean. It would be a waste if we didn't."

"Of course," Sianna replies, using a Magneia charm to draw a plate of cakes towards her, "but one misreading will lead to crippling pain for weeks."

"And I was just thinking how much fun I was having."

"Humour for another time. Sit and enjoy the feast but first activate your Quivvens, helping us to get a closer look at where you're headed."

"The realm of The Winter King," I add, getting a strange look from a witch in hiding.

"Yes, Guppy: a realm about to pivot out of time."

THANKFULLY, SIANNA'S TRUE TO HER WORD — THE QUIVVENS and fountains of remedies detect the tricks weaved into the food. It's not the lesson I thought it was going to be, moving from promises of a feast to struggling with the crushing presence of a blue wall of light, released by a tiny bird with its own unique powers.

There are more lessons to come, probably, but now I'm over the worry of eating myself to death I reach for the cakes nearest to me. I'm surprised at how much time's gone by, the shadow falling over the wall a clock of a different kind. All we need to do now is learn to study the stars, something Sianna brings up soon afterwards.

"When you've had enough to eat, we can move on to the main reason for your visit."

She's really talking to Noah who's still preoccupied with the remaining food, leaving Lucy to nudge him into action.

"The feast is over, lover boy."

"You used to call me angel," Noah jokes through a mouthful of food — maybe not the angel Lucy's looking for after all.

As we wait for him to scoff the sandwiches, I give in to temptation and lean my head back, catching a falling fountain of green remedy, pouring down into the cups that never overspill. I laugh as I gulp the familiar taste of Jysyn Juice, glancing at the sight of Conrad and Lucy doing the same — all to the amusement of our reclusive host and patient Williynx, re-appearing in the tunnel we entered through.

"I can leave you to drink to your heart's content, or we can step into the realm of The Winter King."

That gets my attention, turning away from remedy to possibility: a chance to witness the beauty, danger and majesty of the sky realms.

"I thought we weren't ready to travel there," Lucy challenges, grabbing Noah's arm to move him away from the table.

"Well," Sianna replies with a smile, "there's travelling and *arriving*. Consider it an introduction, allowing you to stand on the axis connecting the S.P.M.A. to the sky realms: a pivoting fortress soon to become a bloody stage."

"War," I utter, already knowing where we're headed.

"Of a certain kind, marking the end of one reign and the beginning of another. It's time; Thylas is waiting to meet you."

With the feast devoured and a bellyful of remedy, I adjust the belt on my black, leather trousers, wondering what a fading king will make of a young Night Ranger with a reputation for battle.

7

CHASING DESTINY

It isn't the stained-glass floor that takes us up to the skies, but a strange seance around the fireplace that crackles as we study the morning sky. We sit in silence for a while, heads lowered with eyes closed as instructed, but nothing happens. Maybe the reclusive lifestyle has got to Sianna — the long, greying hair falling over her shoulders as her bare feet tap rhythmically. Her silver dress is dangerously close to the fire, but this doesn't seem to bother her at all.

Noah's struggling to stay awake, his head dipping every few seconds before he jolts up again.

"I wouldn't fall asleep now," Conrad whispers. "We're just about to get to the juicy part."

"What juicy part would that be?" Noah replies, patting his head to stay alert.

"A storm brewing."

"The only storm's happening in my stomach," Noah adds, adjusting position to release some wind. The look of relief on his face draws a laugh from us and a different response from Sianna: a vision in silver looking up at a motionless sky.

"Take some powder and cover your hands and feet," she instructs as she stands, moving through the living room in a trance-like state.

I shrug at the others, gesturing to the yellow and blue powder scattered across the floor — the powder I saw on my first visit and thought nothing of. "Let's go before she changes her mind," I say to Conrad, Noah and Lucy who all step away from the fire with me, ready to learn the secret of powder and fire.

"Does she mean our shoes or our feet?" Lucy asks, adjusting the hair clip in her cropped, black hair.

"No idea," I reply, "but I'm keeping my shoes on."

"Looks like she's not hanging around for us," Noah comments, gesturing towards the floating figure of Sianna ... rising upwards as the powder is released from her hands ... powder that runs towards the crackling fire.

I grab Conrad by the arm, urging Noah and Lucy to move to the corner of the room ... the very sight I expect to see happening seconds after ... a blast of fire which races across the floor, rising up to Sianna's outstretched hands.

"Be quick or I travel alone," Sianna advises, her greying hair floating around her like a sail directing her course. "The fire and powder will call The Winter King. If the sky responds to the call, we will only have seconds to engage."

That's enough to get us moving, covering our hands and shoes with the yellow and blue powder. There's no time for questions so I wait for the powder to lift me upwards which it does seconds later, guiding me towards the roofless chamber that looks out onto The Royisin Heights.

With Conrad, Noah and Lucy appearing in the air alongside me, we release the powder from our hands, watching as it races towards the fire that roars its response, sending flames darting towards us that we catch with our hands.

Catching fire sounds crazy when you say it, but when you live in a magical universe crazy becomes the norm. The power of the connection is the first thing I notice, the feeling of a lightning bolt surging through me. It's like the feeling you get when activating a charm: a sudden blast of energy propelling you forward.

"Can you see anything?" Conrad asks as the four of us form a circle, the palms of our hands connected to the fire that's acting as our rocket fuel.

"Nothing yet," Lucy replies.

"It's happening," I say, watching as Sianna lifts her hands upwards, whipping the lines of fire like magical ropes controlling an invisible chariot.

"Where?" Noah prompts.

It's more a feeling than a vision, watching our reclusive host orchestrate a path towards Thylas Renn. It's not the way Kaira travelled to the skies in The Goronoff Mountains, but we're entering a new world with new rules to learn, including the multiple modes of travel on offer.

Lightning cracks through the sky seconds later, surging down to connect to Sianna's ropes of fire. It's our turn to connect our ropes of fire to the wild lightning: a connection that fires us upwards. Our powder-covered feet glide along the lightning as if we're ice skating, the ropes of flames controlling our chariot of blazing light.

Thunder follows soon afterwards, adding another dimension to our journey, the rumbling skies releasing a deluge of rain that seems to chase us as we fly along the paths of lightning, keeping track of Sianna.

"Flying on lightning!" Noah shouts out in excitement,

whipping his ropes of fire as if he's at the helm of a carriage, urging his horse forwards.

There's no horse but it gets the same reaction, the lightning sending out sparks of orange light as Noah surges ahead.

"*Yes!*" he shouts as we keep pace with him, Conrad's grey jacket lifting like a cloak as the thunder roars again, suggesting the sky realms are unhappy with our impending visit.

For all we know, the lightning, rain and thunder could be the first line of defence, testing the intention of travelling soldiers. Whatever the reason, it's *a lot of fun*, the rush of exhilaration as we race along the map of lightning at incredible speed — the sight of Laieya appearing in the sky adding a touch of reassurance.

Williynx never leave a Society soldier's side until their safety is ensured, no squawk of concern or blasts of ice suggesting we're in safe hands. As the rain continues to storm towards us like monsters chasing their prey, Sianna vanishes ... the glimmer of silver acting as our beacon disappearing into the storm.

"What now!" Lucy asks as our paths of lightning arc upwards ahead: a sudden vertical ascent leading into darkness.

"We climb higher and find Sianna," I reply, shaking my long, brown hair away from my face. "There's no way we're gaining entry to The Winter King's fortress without her, so let's get a move on."

"That rain doesn't look too friendly," Conrad comments.

"It looks like it's going to swallow us," Noah replies, glancing at his soaked chinos, T-shirt and waistcoat. "They don't do anything *gradually* in the S.P.M.A., do they?"

"I thought you were having fun," Lucy comments, twisting her ropes of fire to manoeuvre closer to Noah.

"I *am*."

"Then stop moaning and get ready to climb through the sky into an abyss."

"Great pep talk."

"Anytime," Lucy replies before she pivots on her path of lightning, spinning in the air to add a little detail to the journey.

I join Lucy, throwing the ropes of light over my head, allowing me to spin through the air ... the map of lightning pivoting with me as the rain roars closer. I think Conrad's right about the rain — it doesn't look friendly — but I've got no plans to get sucked into its vortex.

Returning to an upright position, I speed towards Conrad to plant a kiss on his cheek before hitting the vertical ascent ... four paths of lightning awaiting us ... each in a different colour linked to our penchant stones: a signal of welcome from a fortress in the sky.

With the four of us side-by-side, staying ahead of the roaring rain, we make our ascent as the thunder roars again. I feel my penchant bracelet vibrate as we climb higher, the heat of the ropes of fire increasing as the powder covering my hands fades away. Whatever's waiting for us in the darkness is bound to be spectacular, my mind returning to the glimmering triangle Aarav showed us earlier.

"Not much of a guide, is she?" Noah comments as we feel a sudden force pulling on us. "I prefer my uncle's teaching methods and that's saying something."

"It's all part of the journey," Conrad says as we near the abyss of darkness. "To see how we cope in a new realm of magic. We're Night Rangers, after all, conditioned in finding our way."

"Only there *isn't* a way — just darkness."

"A test of our skill and will, like Conrad said," I add, gripping my ropes of fire tighter as a burning sensation begins. "Night Ranging's comfortable; this won't be so get used to flying into black holes."

"So, do we activate a defensive charm?" Lucy prompts as we near the end of our paths of lightning. "A Velinis charm, maybe, just in case."

"No," I reply. "No charms. We enter on the path offered, and get ready to meet Thylas Renn. Remember, Sianna said our Quivvens would protect us in different ways up here."

"Well, I just hope we get there soon because I need the toilet."

"Thylas should have a few in that massive fortress of his," Conrad comments, kneeling in preparation for the unknown. "Unless you want to go up here. You know, just let loose."

"Grim," Lucy says, pulling a face.

A squawk from Laieya and Erivan gets our attention — our trusted Williynx signalling for us to climb aboard as our pathways of lightning fade away. As we do, I place my hands on Laieya's neck, receiving a gust of cold mist to cool my hands. With the ropes of fire abandoned, we're back to familiar modes of travel, astride our majestic companions as we storm into the realm of The Winter King.

I FIND MYSELF IN A SEPARATE CHANNEL OF DARKNESS SOON after, Laieya gliding silently through what seems to be a portal to an awaiting host. There's no sign of Conrad, Lucy or Noah as I stay low on my Williynx, trying to catch a glimpse of any surrounding life. I feel my penchant bracelet vibrate again, watching as the topaz-blue gemstones light up: a sure sign I'm closing in on the destination.

Sianna's job was to teach us more about the realm of Devreack, dominated by Thylas Renn's white fortress. She's done this in her own way, providing us with the tools to travel before leaving us to make our own way. No one needs their hand held anymore, so we'll be treated like any other soldier on a mission beyond The Society Sphere — with consideration and suspicion.

Society elders deal with underage wizards in different ways. Some keep their distance, others offer guidance and then there are those who make their resentment clear — like the two Domitus we had a run in with a while ago.

As I press my face into Laieya's powder-blue feathers, I wonder what Thylas Renn's response is going to be when he finally meets us: a legendary soldier aware of the dangers of an awkward transition of power.

Taeia comes to mind again as Laieya spreads her wings, releasing a cloud of white mist which forms into its own portal ... this one providing a vision of a colossal, white building ... rotating on an invisible axis ... the anchor providing a stabilising force. The next thing I see is Conrad, Lucy and Noah kneeling on separate paths leading to the white fortress, their Williynx resting proudly beside them.

I remember being told of the hundred paths stretching out from The Winter King's fortress, but seeing it is something else. The fortress is the size of ten football fields, rising higher than any stadium I've ever seen and anchored to nothing but the sky it floats in.

As Laieya reduces in form to glide through the portal of white mist, I sit up on my feathered companion, blinking as the intense white light floods in: the sight of an enormous white Williynx perched on the top of the fortress giving me a sense of being *elsewhere.*

I've arrived in the realm of Devreack: home of The Winter King and the beginning of a new adventure.

8

NEW REALMS

As I rest on the rotating axis in the sky with Laieya perched proudly alongside me, I look across to Conrad, Lucy and Noah who stay in their kneeling positions. Conrad gives me a reassuring nod, although there's little to go on to make a Night Ranger feel at home.

With the massive, white Williynx remaining on top of the white fortress, a colossal guard to a prized asset, the only other sign of movement are the rotating paths that stretch around Thylas Renn's kingdom — one hundred arms of protection keeping intruders at bay.

There's no sign of Sianna which doesn't help either, suggesting she's already made herself at home in The Winter King's fortress. The others are too far away to communicate with, the white paths separated by some distance, and I get the feeling now isn't the time to call out to them. Silence hangs in the air, our kneeling figures hoping for a friendly welcome.

With Laieya keeping her head lowered, following the tradition of respect on entering a royal realm, I glance at the scars on my wrists, wondering how long it's going to be before I get new ones. The scars don't bother me anymore — medals from my first year in the S.P.M.A.

The first signal of movement comes from our Williynx, lifting their heads as they spread their wings, releasing feathers as they do so. The feathers fall onto the paths the four of us kneel on, sending a line of colour running along them towards the faceless fortress in the sky.

I glance at the others as our Williynx take to the sky, the coloured pathways stretching upwards. Now each of us is surrounded by a protective wall of light, mine powder-blue with Conrad's silhouette visible within his turquoise wall of light.

With Noah and Lucy gesturing everything's okay, the signal to move towards the fortress is given by the enormous, white Williynx which rises into the air in a sign of welcome, sending out a fine mist of ice that rests on our channels of light.

The mist hovers at the end of my illuminated path, similar to the one Laieya created when we flew into position earlier. The only difference is the way it interacts with the wall of light, lifting it like a curtain at the end to reveal an entrance that goes on and on ... the sight of a friendly face making me feel a *lot* better about arriving in a strange kingdom.

Kaira stands alongside Sianna, waving me on which is all the encouragement I need. With our Williynx offering encouraging noises from above, I keep pace with the others as we make our way into a fortress burdened by an unknown fate. It's hard to believe Taeia Renn will be the lord of this manor soon, but unless he does something *mad* we'll have to kneel in his presence in the future. I bet he'll *love* that.

I meet Conrad, Lucy and Noah as we reach the entrance to Thylas Renn's palace in the sky — the four of us glancing back at the walls of colour shimmering around us. Kaira waits at the end of the long passageway, gesturing for us to step closer. As far as I can tell, there are no windows or doors on this alabaster palace in the sky, although that means little when you've got magic at your disposal.

"Why do we need four paths if we're all heading in the same direction?" Noah queries.

"Maybe we're not," Conrad replies. "We don't know how things work up here, so let's just go with it until we do."

"Kaira looks taller," Lucy comments as we prepare to enter our individual doorways of light.

It's the first time I've noticed this ... my best friend standing at the same height as Sianna. Her growth spurt is another mystery to be discussed, but first it's time to meet another legendary Renn and find out more about our part in an uncertain destiny.

"Come on," I say. "Kaira's waiting for us."

It's enough to get us moving, each taking a step through our doorway of light, ready to come face to face with a king in crisis.

"You've grown," I say to Kaira as I reach my best friend, giving her a hug.

"Must be the sky air," Kaira replies with the warm smile I've missed.

"You found your way," Sianna adds, regal and mysterious as she stands alongside Kaira.

I nod, realising sarcasm won't do me any favours. It's a test, after all, being prepared to travel here: a test offered by Casper, Aarav and Sianna. Three of us have fought in war and two haven't, so this feels like the first step towards judgement — whether we're going to be equipped for what lies beyond Devreack and the faceless fortress we're standing in.

There isn't much to see except for the pathway that seems to stretch on forever — onwards and upwards like a never-ending tunnel to nowhere. It obviously goes somewhere and I imagine Kaira's here to act as our friendly guide. She's a lot more relaxed than Sianna, that's for sure, whose method of teaching seems to be of the silent variety.

"Everyone okay?" Kaira asks as Sianna glances at nothing in particular.

"Better now we're here," Conrad replies, rubbing the scar on his neck.

"Thylas is waiting for us. Good to see you've activated your Quivvens."

I glance at the soft, blue light glowing in my wrist — my Quivven placed near my penchant bracelet: dual protection against an unknown enemy. Sianna reinforced the need to keep our Quivvens active, helping us to detect deception on our travels.

She also mentioned we've got the Jacqus in the wings if needed: the magical, blue birds who'll offer us a path to safety when danger strikes. There's no danger at present, so I relax and study my surroundings.

"It's a bit of a walk but we can talk on the way," Kaira adds, giving me a nudge as we make our way along the endless pathway.

It's a friendly gesture reminding me of old times, when life was simpler and full of more innocent wonder. We formed a bond then which returns each time we meet: a bond that extends to Jacob and Conrad, soon to incorporate Lucy and Noah.

It's a unity that got us through a lot of scrapes in the past, helping us to unravel dark mysteries. With Kaira and Conrad walking alongside me, it feels like old times again: a young band of Society soldiers ready to face a new enemy in the skies.

LIGHT BEGINS TO FLOOD IN AS WE MAKE OUR WAY ALONG THE pathway — a shifting light that moves with us as if it's assessing our intentions. Protective measures are common in all realms so this is nothing to worry about, leaving me to study the strange marks cut into the white alabaster stone.

The marks are like the ones I saw in the underground world of The Royisin Heights. Conrad runs his hand along the marks, moving closer to the wall on our right as we head along the pathway, inching closer to a fateful meeting.

"They look ancient," he comments, causing Sianna to turn towards him.

"They're as old as our magical world," our silver-draped guide replies, "containing secrets and spells."

"Can you read the marks?" Lucy asks.

"Only a Winter King hears the secrets carved in the stone: secrets helping them to see all things."

"Hears?"

"Yes, like whispers across time."

"Helping them to maintain balance up here," I comment.

"Precisely, Guppy, but this must wait for another time. First we need to step through a window."

"*Through* it?" Noah queries as a massive window glimmers into life.

A flock of Williynx fly past the window, enjoying a break from Society duty. I'm beginning to wonder if The Winter King actually exists, moving closer to Kaira as we walk on. "How do you like it up here?" I ask my friend who offers me a familiar smile.

"I like it just fine," Kaira replies, sharing the beauty and serenity of her aunt. "My dad says it's another piece of my past and a way to explore new places."

"So, you're not really returning?"

"Yes and no. I want to help but don't want to be tied down."

"Like a free agent."

"Something like that," Kaira replies.

"Well, I'm glad you're here to keep us company," I say as we move towards the enormous window.

"The best company I could hope for," Kaira replies, standing a little taller than me now.

She's added a little sophistication to her style from two years ago — the velvet, blue jacket adding a nice touch to the jeans and shoes. I'm happy with my all-black outfit for now, although I wonder if it's going to draw unwanted attention soon. It's hardly a uniform of someone minding their own business, maybe not the best strategy when we venture beyond The Winter King's fortress.

"We're here," Sianna states as the large window moves towards us ... liquid glass contained by a stone frame formed in an arch: a portal leading to a royal sanctuary. "When the window makes contact keep moving," Sianna instructs. "It works like The Web of Azryllis, assessing our intentions. The highest ranking witches and wizards have similar protective measures."

Kaira smiles at the sight of me holding my breath, linking arms with me as the liquid glass forms over our faces ... reminding me of a much less-friendly curse that filled the lungs with venom ... the Niavak curse that took Smyck's life.

"You need to breathe it in," Kaira explains, offering a reassuring nod.

"Breathe in *glass*?" Noah comments in his typically dramatic way.

"Think of it as a Nivrium," Kaira adds, "or imagine you're standing in the waters of Gilweean. It's the same principle, designed to assess the temperature of things."

"Quickly," Sianna encourages as Noah's face turns a worrying shade of red. "It's harmless unless it senses significant resistance."

As Noah's fear gets the better of him, Lucy gives him a helpful slap on the back which causes him to cough. As he does, the liquid film over his face enters his mouth, bringing about a touch of comedy as Noah doubles over in anticipation of sudden pain.

"Are you sure he's ready for this?" Kaira asks as we step through the portal of liquid glass.

"No," I reply with a strained expression, drawing a laugh from us both.

With Lucy and Noah through, followed by Sianna, we watch as our mode of transport fades away, offering no vision of white Williynx or fading kings ... until the ceiling lowers ... a stage fit for a king who appears in glittering, grey robes. White is the only other colour in evidence — the white beard and white eyes making the enormous figure look like a blind visionary.

"He looks like a killer," Noah whispers as his nerves get the better of him.

"Here," Conrad says, offering his friend a vial of green liquid: Jysyn Juice when courage is in short supply.

I've got no doubt Noah will find the courage needed on this quest, just like I did when a lethal artefact got everyone's attention a while ago. It's not every day you meet a magical messiah, after all, so I stay close to Kaira as Thylas Renn's concrete stage touches down, leaving the introductions to Sianna who walks over to take his hand.

I doubt Thylas is troubled by the appearance of a few kids in his castle, turning his white eyes onto us. It's strange being stared at by someone who looks blind. Whatever he senses he keeps to himself, turning to Kaira to complete the introductions.

As Noah gets a grip on his fear, we follow Kaira's instruction to stay put until we're called forward, eventually receiving the royal gesture from a mountain of a man, about to introduce us to a whole new world of wonder in the skies.

9

THE WINTER KING

Thylas Renn's white eyes are hypnotic, drawing you into the powerful energy field surrounding him. He doesn't move, looking straight at us from his stage of concrete that rose down from the ceiling. Strange arrivals aren't anything new but kings are, so I keep a handle on my impulsive nature, deciding patience is the name of the game.

The silence gets uncomfortable after a while, Lucy glancing over to me as if I know what's going on. I haven't got a clue what the tradition is here so keep an eye on Kaira, trusting she's spent long enough in Thylas Renn's company to know the rhythm of things.

Noah steps forward to offer a hand which goes down badly — *very* badly. The towering figure turns his white eyes on Noah, a look of rage forming on his face which makes our friend retreat quickly, reaching in his trouser pockets for another vial of Jysyn Juice.

"Just stay still, will you?" Conrad whispers, annoyed at Noah's edginess.

We're guests here, after all, studying every gesture until we've grasped the way of things. The only issue is we don't have anything to go on right now, standing in the presence of a colossal man with trouble on his mind. I've met some intense wizards in my time — Casper Renn and Aarav Khan to name two — but this particular wizard is something else.

He's the size of a Ulux — the ageing giants from Sad Souls — but far broader as if he's grown to fit the scale of his kingdom. This makes me think of Kaira's sudden growth spurt, making me wonder if *time* operates differently up here. I mean, a giant of a king and a friend who's suddenly taller than me.The thought trails off as our royal host finally offers some words.

"Your shoes," Thylas Renn states. "Remove them."

With the stage of concrete beginning to rise slowly, I follow the others and do as I'm told. Sianna is already bare footed, like she was on our first visit to The Royisin Heights.

Touch and time, I think as the concrete stage returns to the ceiling it descended from: the importance of touch and time in a royal chamber that feels more like a prison cell. This thought fades as we rise higher, entering a glass tower looking out over a faltering universe.

"An axis of a different kind," Kaira whispers as we step into the hexagonal space decorated with a hundred windows: one for each of the pathways surrounding The Winter King's Fortress.

It reminds me of the illustrated windows in the S.P.M.A., offering a glimpse of other Society faculties — another surveillance device to keep the peace. The tower of glass rotates slowly ... one way then the other ... slats of glass to spy through, reminding me of the shards of glass decorating the walls of Sianna's home in The Royisin Heights.

Like Sianna, our towering host uses them to study the universe he reigns over. I see towering, teetering buildings: flatlands ravaged by the wind and weeds weaved into delicate dwellings. Caverns ravaged by fire catch my eye in the window nearest to me, including the thing I've been waiting to see: a striking, immaculately dressed group seeking blood.

"Bloodseekers," Conrad whispers.

He's unusually quiet in the presence of a mysterious legend but, then again, so is everyone else — each of us careful not to touch the glass we peer through.

"A simple touch takes you to your desired location, but there is much to master first," Thylas Renn comments, looking directly at me. "You need to be in tune with every element you come into contact with, both harmless and fatal."

"The reason we've taken our shoes off," Noah adds, flinching as The Winter King steps towards him. "Material magic is the art to be mastered in the sky realms: charms created from what exists as opposed to what doesn't."

"So, manipulating things," Lucy adds, looking a little concerned as Thylas Renn places his hands near Noah's head.

"Indeed, Miss Flint — manipulating things both human and inanimate. Sianna has forged a path for you on this journey, but there will be no adult guide managing more sinister forces aiming to persuade, weaken or obliterate you. Therefore, we first need to train our minds without the aid of the remedies you rely on: they will offer no protection here."

"So, what protection do we have?" Conrad asks, turning away from the window looking at the groups hunting blood.

"Your Quivven and penchant have a combined power:

material objects releasing a unique power when used together. This power relies on your ability to harness the power hidden in the skies: ancient power offered to the blessed and brave."

"Like learning magic all over again," I comment.

"Discovering what's already within you, Guppy," Sianna replies, speaking for the first time.

She hasn't left Thylas' side since we arrived, adding to the sense they're an item, although I don't see Thylas as the romantic type — the way he stares *right through* things. I want to ask about his white eyes but know it isn't the right time, so decide to stay focused on our journey here.

"Well, we seemed to navigate our chariots of fire to get here okay."

"The first lesson in manipulating material elements," Thylas adds.

"Fire and powder."

"Fire and lightning, Guppy," Kaira adds, uttering 'Smekelin' to release a ball of fire into the air.

As the glass tower continues to rotate slowly, I watch as Kaira allows the fireball to rise upwards, attaching itself to each window frame. "Fire is a defensive charm we generate when in danger, but we've never used it as a neutral weapon."

"Neutral?" Lucy queries.

"Helping us outside of battle. You're called The Fire Witch because of the way you appear through fire, and the Smekelin charm is used to attack. Now, you've travelled through the skies with ropes of fire, riding lightning as you whipped up speed through the air.

In the sky realms, *everything* holds magic — normal, everyday things from fire to powder and lightning. It's less about creating magic out of thin air, and more about using what's at your disposal."

"So, Society magic won't work up here?" Noah prompts.

"*Both* will work, Master Khan," Thylas replies, "but only when you've learned to be at one with each element. You've learned to ride lightning without harm and wrap your hands in fire to light up the skies. Now, you need to understand the power and danger of mixing magical laws: the Society's and ours."

"Just in case it backfires," I add.

"Less backfiring than *engulfing*. The skies are alive with wonder and wickedness: the same delicate balance you've helped to restore. The tornados of rain chasing you were a mirage of my own making, but be in no doubt that monsters live up here — some in human form and others not."

"Bloodseekers," Conrad comments, returning his attention to the elegant crowd roaming for the dead.

"Relatively harmless," Thylas replies, "As you know, I have drunk blood for many years, helping me to maintain my strength and extend my years. Time has decided my final destination, however, leading to the puzzle of a distant relative: the reason you're here."

"Taeia," Noah says, touching the sides of his head as he does.

It's the place Thylas placed his hands, pressing them against Noah's black hair without a word of explanation. The way Noah's touching his head suggests he thinks something's been planted in there: a royal blessing tinted with a special type of magic just for him.

"Is he definitely going to be the next Winter King?" I ask.

"A king of sorts ... for the winters are notoriously bleak in Devreack, bleaching your soul until you're pure of restless intentions. Few humans can stand the cold ... a cold that seeps into the bones and blisters the skin ... the reason we stand in a barren space."

"So, you're alone up here?"

"In some ways but not in others. I have the sky for company and creatures who never leave my side. Also, a Winter King is blessed with 'blind sight' once his pilgrimage is complete: the prize for becoming pure of spirit."

"Is that why you've got white eyes?" I ask, finally plucking up the courage.

"White eyes, a white beard and blinding visions: the mark of a man who has survived seven winters. Many heirs to the throne of Devreack perish on their travels, having to roam through every region of the sky realms, battling enemies and their own demons until a Williynx sheds its natural colour, bleeding itself into the land to mark the end of a seven-year pilgrimage."

"Sounds a bit intense," Noah comments, still touching his head as if he's got a secret locked in there.

"It's the cost of ruling a kingdom," Thylas adds, clapping his hands in Noah's direction, "and no rare thing is earned easily. Kaira has earned my trust partly due to our family allegiance, but also because of the part some of you played in a recent battle. Your gifts are rare and commitment impressive, but be clear that you have entered uncharted territory."

"You said a simple touch takes you to the desired location," Conrad asks as Noah grabs onto Lucy, grimacing as he shakes his head.

"What's wrong with him?"

"His first test," Kaira comments, deciding to break her silence. She takes out a vial of Liqin from her blue, velvet jacket. "As Thylas mentioned earlier, Society remedies won't solve problems up here, so we all need to pass some tests before the journey really begins."

"What does he need to do?" Conrad prompts, glancing between Kaira, Sianna and Thylas.

"Adapt or return to familiar ground," Sianna replies in her typically unhelpful way.

"Meaning?" Lucy asks with an obvious degree of concern.

"Meaning using what's at his disposal," Kaira offers.

"Which is *what*...?"

"Blood," I reply, instinctively knowing it makes sense. "Thylas drinks it to maintain his strength and extend his life, so it's harmless: a human remedy we never knew existed."

Noah shakes his head at the thought, but the pain isn't getting any better. He drops to his knees as if he's in the grips of a fever, looking up at Thylas who watches on without a trace of concern.

It's obvious he doubts Noah's capacity to handle what's up here, but unity is what binds us so I take charge, uttering 'Comeuppance'.

With the Vaspyl in my hands, I throw it into the air, watching as it turns into a small knife.

"Here," I say to Lucy, realising Noah's in no fit state to use a blade on his skin. "Just a small cut ... enough to draw blood then it's up to him."

Lucy nods, steadying Noah as he writhes on the floor. With a steady hand, she rests the knife on his upper fore-arm. "Night Rangers turning into vampires," she mutters sarcastically as she draws blood, wiping it with her fingers and offering it to Noah who still refuses.

"Just bloody taste it, will you!" Conrad urges, taking the vial of Liqin from Kaira. "It's your own blood or a remedy that won't work. You had a choice to come up here, remember, so get on with it or we're leaving."

With that, Noah tastes the blood on Lucy's fingers, resting his head back on the floor when he's done. "Leaving?" he mutters in Conrad's direction. "Anywhere where we can ride lightning has got my vote."

"Good," Conrad replies, sensing his friend's humour returning, "so stop whinging and stand up. We're in the presence of a king, after all."

The blood seems to do the trick because Noah's back on his feet in no time, shying away from the offer of more from Lucy.

"How does it taste?" she asks.

"Like my blood," Noah replies with a sarcastic smile. "I don't want to kill anybody yet, though, so that's probably a good thing. By the way, what's the difference between drinking blood for strength and becoming a Bloodseeker?"

"The path you choose," Thylas adds, stroking his white beard as the glittering, grey robes lift over his bare feet. "Only the pure can drink blood for strength and longevity; everyone else becomes a predator of the dead."

"A bit like Melackin in our world," Kaira explains, realising she's referred to my mum. "Sorry, Guppy. I didn't mean to ..."

"It's fine," I say, ignoring the emotion rising in me. "Mum made her own choices like all Melackin have, although I'm working on things with her with Jacob's help."

"I miss Jacob," Kaira adds.

"Me too, although Jacob's got his own part to play with Taeia."

"Ultimately, it will be Jacob who senses Taeia's path to the skies," Sianna states, blowing the remaining powder from her hand, directing it towards the window dominated by a blood-red sky. "Until then, we will venture through our glass tower, learning to map energy and connect with all material things at our disposal: the laws of magic in the sky realms."

"So, we just *walk* through the glass?" Lucy asks.

"Through the glass and into a brooding sky," Thylas adds. "Where your journey begins."

10

SKY ATLAS

The sky we step onto covers our feet like a protective floor, separating us from what's below. I feel the surge of energy running through my legs the moment I step through the tower of glass — a sensation I struggle to get used to until Kaira tells me to relax and give into it.

"It's all part of mapping the energy up here," my friend says, offering me a smile as she lifts her feet from the carpet of clouds surrounding them. "Our bare feet help us to form a bond with the sky realm we've entered, although this is just a test."

"How do you mean?" Conrad asks, sticking by my side as Thylas and Sianna wait for us up ahead.

"Every one of the hundred paths is a protective barrier, stopping enemies entering. Remember how you had to bow when you arrived here?"

The four of us nod, circling around Kaira as she explains more. "Thylas sees everything that goes on in Devreack, either through his tower of glass or by closing his eyes."

"It's strange how he looks blind," Lucy adds. "What did

he say about his soul being bleached by a seven-year pilgrimage?"

"The pilgrimage all Winter Kings have to take to prove their worth."

"And a lot of heirs to the throne fail," Noah adds, lifting his right foot out of the bank of dark clouds. The string of light surrounding his feet makes him feel reassured we're not about to plunge to our deaths. "Well, that's what Thylas said, anyway."

"Right, Noah," Kaira adds, buttoning her blue, velvet jacket as the wind whips around us. "Those that complete the pilgrimage are purified of all 'restless thoughts'. The final stage is the bleaching of the soul — the reason for Thylas' white eyes and beard."

"How does a white Williynx link to all this again?" Conrad asks, kneeling to catch a glimpse of indistinct shapes below.

"A Williynx bleeds out its natural colour," Kaira explains. "Williynx are pure so can be trusted to assess the secrets of a human heart."

"Anyway, back to Thylas being able to see by closing his eyes," I prompt, wanting to learn more about the magical laws of the sky realms. "Does he use a Quivven like we do?"

Kaira shakes her head, spinning slowly on our carpet of clouds. It's a random gesture that gets a smile from us all: a reminder of how young she still is in a world of adult drama. "Once you're enthroned as The Winter King, you're given two gifts: the secrets scribed into the walls of the fortress and the gift of 'blind sight'."

"So, the same as using a Quivven to fight blind?" Noah asks.

"In some ways," Kaira replies, suggesting we catch up with the waiting figures of Thylas and Sianna: a mystery all to themselves. "The main difference is the Quivven can only illuminate the realm you're in; a Winter King can see one hundred realms at once: a blessing and a burden that stays with them for life."

"Why does Thylas need both?" Lucy asks. "I mean, if the scribblings on the wall and his white eyes help him see his whole kingdom, why not just be blessed with one?"

Kaira spins again, pirouetting like a ballet dancer. "Because one gives him a vision of the present, and the other a vision of the future — the last thing we want to fall into the hands of Taeia Renn."

"Because he's unlikely to do good things with the gift," I say, already seeing carnage about to unfold when Taeia takes his place on the throne of Devreack.

"Really bad things probably, going by everything I've heard."

"So, we need to stop him," Lucy comments.

"Easier said than done," Kaira adds, "because Taeia's unlikely to pass the seven-year pilgrimage let along *go on it*."

"You think he's about to go AWOL?" Noah queries, deciding to add a spin of his own.

"That's what a Nivrium is telling us, and the waters of Gilweean."

"And the Renns are water readers," I say, offering my friend a smile.

"So, we wait for the mayhem to begin," Conrad adds, deciding to touch the strands of light surrounding his feet. The shock he gets sends him flat on his back, sinking into the dark clouds before Kaira comes to his rescue, uttering 'Magneia' to draw the energy away from Conrad's feet and towards her.

Before we know it, Kaira's got lightning pouring out of her hands — a force that makes her hair stand on end as

Conrad is lifted to his feet. His hands and feet connect to a blizzard of light, like the one on our race through the skies.

This is different, though, because there was no lightning on offer this time; Kaira's *created it* from the string of light around Conrad's feet. It's obviously the first lesson in material magic: the art of combining Society spells with what's at hand.

"Clever," I comment, leading Kaira to take a bow.

With a laugh from us all, she adds. "Trust me, that's nothing. We're going to learn to catch the lightning now, channelling it through our bodies before finding out more about what's happening below. It's a different feeling to using the Promesiun charm because the force is outside of us, not within us."

"More powerful?" Lucy poses.

"*Much* more powerful," Kaira adds, "and less stable so get ready for some new scars."

WITH OUR FIRST LESSON ON MATERIAL MAGIC ABOUT TO BEGIN, we join Thylas and Sianna further along the carpet of brooding clouds. There are no Williynx to keep us company this time, making me wonder where Laieya and our other feathered companions are.

The way they raced past the window makes me think they're having their own fun, currently unburdened of human problems. Trouble seems to land at the S.P.M.A.'s doorstep in one form or another, meaning it won't be long before Conrad returns to the art of sky riding, leading a new army into battle.

I can't keep my eyes off Thylas Renn's massive frame whenever I'm close to him. There's also his age which is a bit of a mystery. Kaira referred to him as her 'great, great, great something or other' as a joke. Whatever the family connection, it seems to be on good terms as the king of the skies nods for Kaira to continue her lesson.

"Magic's about learning rhythms as much as activating it at the right time," Kaira says, holding a ball of lightning in each hand.

It's the casual way she goes about the lesson that impresses me: a sign she's grown in more than physical stature recently. Unlike us, Kaira's already becoming at one with the brooding sky of Devreack, her bare feet surrounded by surges of lightning as she continues.

I can already picture her as an adult, looking a lot like her aunt as she guides young witches and wizards through their paces. I see her teaching in The Cendryll, alongside Jacob who'd be happy to have a friendly face, helping him to manage the mayhem of youth. Maybe it's wishful thinking or maybe I've got my own way of reading the future — not a water reader or a Winter King, just a girl relying on instincts.

It's my instincts that kick me into action now, whispering 'Magneia' to draw the strings of light towards me. The blast of energy that rises shoots past my face, making Lucy and Noah duck. Conrad's joined me in the desire to master material magic, repeatedly saying, 'Magneia' each time the magnetic charm fails to control the lightning fizzing around us.

"It's not about controlling the force, but working with it," Sianna offers, returning to her role as mystical guide.

She joins our circle of five, leaving Thylas Renn to lift his hands to the heavens ... as if he's got something else in store for us.

"How do you work with lightning blasting past your face?" I ask.

"By connecting to it as it does, Guppy. Remember, you have to become at one with a particular energy before we travel beyond the safe confines of this fortress."

"But we're not in the fortress," Noah comments before he ducks out of harm's way again. "Maybe practice a bit *further away*," he says in my direction. "I'm not anti scars, but I'd prefer to get them from a mess of my own making."

"Well, you're going to have to make a mess to master what's up here," Conrad replies, stamping his bare feet as the strings of light transform into blue flames.

"Choose the charm to mitigate the force of the flames," Thylas instructs, brushing past me and Kaira as Conrad jumps from foot to foot, blowing on the blue fire covering his bare feet.

At the sight of Lucy and Noah activating a Levenan charm, Thylas swings his right arm towards them ... a gesture that sends them into the skies ... their legs hanging above them as they shout out for help. "Ignorance will get you killed so heed this warning: Society charms have no power unless *connected* to a material property, so connect to the tornado of rain to prove your worth."

As Noah and Lucy swim in mid-air, Conrad and I try to ignite the lightning once more, ready to grab on before it blasts past us.

"Remember, it's about *connection* not control," Kaira comments as she stretches the balls of lightning into a frame of light around her.

Now it looks like she's standing in a picture frame: a famous witch frozen in time. As her hair lifts under the force of the contained lightning, she reinforces the point of unity once more.

"It was our bond that gave us the advantage last time, but the bond you need to make this time is with the *elements*. The easiest way to understand the sky realms is to imagine everything as equal to you: clouds, lightning, stars and thunder."

"Can you get us *down* from here!" Noah shouts as thunder rumbles through the sky, signalling another chase on the cards.

His request is ignored by the towering figure of Thylas. His raised hands make it look like he's called the thunder: a god of magic conducting an orchestra of sorts, although not the sort Lucy and Noah had in mind.

A Fixilia charm — or something like it — keeps them hanging upside down in mid-air, and it doesn't look like things are going to improve for them ... the sight of a winged creature formed from a blizzard of rain surging towards them.

"It's a creature released from a Zombul," Conrad comments without his usual degree of confidence. "Got to be. Unless ..."

"Unless Thylas wants to make short work of the meek," Sianna states, dipping her bare feet into the bank of clouds as if she's by the ocean.

This is no ocean and there's no paradise in sight, so I park my failed attempts at controlling lightning, turning my attention to the creature released by thunder: a winged illusion or a genuine threat? As Thylas whips the sky into a frenzy, I get the feeling Kaira's the one to ask for help.

"Well, what do they do?" Conrad asks, beating me to it.

"What Thylas has told them to do," Kaira replies, gesturing for the two of us to step into her frame of lightning. "Think of it as a bubble of protection."

"Like the Velinis charm which won't work up here," I add, trusting Kaira's choice as I always have.

"How did you make the frame?"

"Combining Society magic with the things at hand," Kaira replies as the rain pelts down, falling onto the frame of lightning but not on us.

"It sounds simple when you say it like that," Conrad replies, happy his feet aren't covered in blue flames anymore.

"It's simpler than you think," Kaira adds. "It's a matter of altering your perception."

"How do you mean?"

"Your feet weren't burnt by the blue fire, and the lightning bolt that knocked you on your back hasn't hurt you."

"Because...?"

"Because a bond has been formed here, Conrad — similar to the bond the Society has with its creatures."

"So, you mean the lightning's on our side?" I prompt, reaching out to touch the fizzing frame untouched by the rain.

"Exactly, Guppy. Think of it like mounting a Williynx for the first time; you have to form a bond before trust is developed and then *you're off*."

"So, it's back to following our instincts?"

"Yes. Let your instincts guide you like they have before. The Grayling clan might not be energy readers, but you are. You're the one that sensed danger during your first few days in the S.P.M.A. If you can work that out, you can work out how to manage a bit of lightning."

"It's that *thing* I'm worried about," Conrad says, pointing to the winged creature closing in on Lucy and Noah.

"What would you use if you were stuck up there?" Sianna asks, standing directly under Lucy and Noah.

"The Smekelin charm," Conrad replies. "I'd connect the fire charm to the lightning around us, flooding the creature with a powerful blast to send it packing."

"Well, what are you waiting for? Thylas has no intention of calling off the creature, so I'd suggest you put your plan into action."

"You're joking...?" I ask, but it's clear Sianna *isn't* joking, making me wonder if a trip to the sky realms was a good idea after all.

Conrad doesn't waste any time on doubt, uttering 'Smekelin' as he reaches out to capture handfuls of lightning. His copper-blonde hair stands on end as he does, the shocked expression reflecting the energy field he's trying to contain.

"Come on then!" he says to Kaira and me. "Together."

Kaira nods, asking us to kneel before she re-shapes the frame of lightning we're standing in. As we do, she turns it into an arrow shape, releasing the arrow of fire-tinged lightning towards Lucy and Noah.

Luckily, our friends have faith in our plan, reaching out to capture the arrow of lightning as it surges towards them.

"Pivot and fire!" Kaira shouts towards them, putting her hands together to imitate firing a gun.

Instincts are exactly what we need now, just like Kaira said: the instincts we need to trust before stepping into unfamiliar realms. Lucy and Noah mouth the Magneia charm, catching the arrow of fire lightning as it reaches them.

They use the force of its trajectory to pivot upright, shouting 'Promesiun' to blast the arrow of fire-tinged lightning towards the enormous, bat-like creature that explodes into black rain.

As our friends touch back down on our carpet of clouds,

we find ourselves attached to a different energy field: one fit for a king. Whatever's dragging us towards Thylas is invisible, although it feels like chains dragging our ankles and wrists.

I look at Kaira for an explanation but her eyes are on the faint glimmering in the sky. As we're dragged closer to The Winter King, the force field binding us becomes visible: a maze of light linked to our hands, hearts and feet.

"This is getting weird," Noah comments as Thylas taps his feet on the stage of clouds.

"You're standing in a magical universe in the skies," Lucy counters. "*Of course* it's weird."

"It feels like we're being ordained," Conrad comments as the force field pulls on our skin, like it did when Aarav Khan put Taeia in his place.

"You are, sort of," Kaira explains. "A blood bond is being forged."

"With whose blood?"

"Ours — the reason our skin's stretching."

"He knows how to make people feel welcome, doesn't he?" Noah says, returning to his habit of sarcasm.

"Well, he's a lot more welcoming than what's *down there*."

"Which is?" I ask.

"Kelph," Kaira adds. "Run by pirates and surrounded by Bloodseekers."

"When do we jump in?" Noah adds with a smile.

"Be careful what you wish for," Kaira replies, offering me the look I've missed the most: a sign there's plenty of adventure in her yet.

11

BLOOD BONDS

The blood bond is the way unity is formed between magicians and the sky — or at least that's what it looks like. With a sense of what's waiting for us below our carpet of clouds, I ready myself for a blood ritual. It's not long before our feet lift from the ground ... only a few inches but enough to complete a web of bloodlines formed around us.

I'm surprised at how painless it is, watching as an invisible thread pulls at my skin, drawing blood as it does so. The blood stretches out in a perfect line, connecting with Kaira's then Conrad's, Lucy's and finally Noah's. The centre of this blood bond is, of course, the king of the castle ... Thylas Renn ... standing with outstretched arms as if he's drawing his disciples towards him.

He's a messiah of sorts, although he wears his power lightly like all Renns. There's something *regal* about them all, including Kaira who stands alongside me, focused on the job at hand as we hover above our platform of clouds. The blue, velvet jacket makes her look older — as does the growth spurt that I'm still puzzled by.

Thylas is a giant and the white Williynx guarding his fortress three times the size of the majestic creatures gracing the S.P.M.A. As we circle our host, ready for the next phase of our journey, I glance at Conrad who rubs his neck where his Quivven is buried.

An outline of blood surrounds the deep, blue glow of his Quivven: an omen of sorts. I decide to return my attention to Thylas, studying the bloodlines as we begin to spin closer, ribbons of blood wrapping around us before we touch down again.

I don't feel any different but know a layer of protection's been added — a protection that marks us all in different ways.

"Are you okay, Guppy?" Conrad asks, rubbing at the outline of blood around his Quivven.

"Why?"

"Your eyes ... they're bloodshot. I can barely see your pupils."

"Is your vision affected?" Kaira asks, showing me three fingers then five: a joke to reassure me everything's okay.

"I can see fine," I say, sensing now isn't the time for vanity. A quick flip of a Vaspyl would give me a mirror to check out my new look, but I'm guessing we've got more important things to sort out than bloodshot eyes.

"It's your blood mark," Kaira explains, nodding towards Sianna whose own mark is around her neck.

"What are they for? Protection?"

"Yes; it marks the part of your body to protect."

"From an attack?"

"Yep," Kaira adds. "Your blood mark moves with each sky realm you travel to."

"And we're headed to Kelph where Bloodseekers are

waiting to welcome us," Noah says, scanning his body for his blood mark.

"There," Lucy says, pointing to a red dot under Noah's chin.

"Great," Noah comments, rubbing the mark. "I've got being knifed in the throat to look forward to."

"Always so dramatic," Lucy adds, pointing to her heart before saying, "We could trade. It looks like I'm going to get my heart ripped out."

"And we signed up for this," Noah replies, shaking his black hair out of his eyes as he utters 'Magneia', deciding now would be a good time to test his ability to capture lightning.

It's a success, Noah smiling as the threads of lightning spark and explode around his hands: a positive sign our blood bond has formed the hoped-for unity with the skies of Devreack.

"Maybe they've got it wrong and I'm the real heir," Noah jokes. "I mean, who would you rather have as your king: me or Taeia?"

"*Our* king?" Conrad replies, rolling his eyes at his friend's excited state. "I think the lightning's gone to your head."

"Well, it feels good — like a tornado running through your veins."

"Excellent," Kaira adds, capturing her own lightning bolts before adding, "because lighting's how we're getting *down there*."

"To Kelph?" Lucy asks, jumping as Thylas and Sianna draw a shower of surging light towards them, their arms raised upwards as if they're calling on the graces of ancient sky gods.

"Yes, so capture what you can because we're about to vanish through the clouds."

It's enough to kick Lucy and Conrad into action, each using the Magneia charm to draw chariots of lightning towards them — just like we did on our way up here. The only difference is there are no ropes of fire, making me wonder if I'm about to experience a new type of free fall.

It's strange travelling to unknown realms without our Williynx, leaving them behind to protect a king's fortress while he's gone. I doubt it's just a group of Williynx defending Thylas' kingdom; the strange scribblings on the fortress' walls probably transforming the white palace into a crippling maze for any unwelcome guests.

"Guppy, let's go," Conrad prompts, getting my attention with a shower of light.

As Thylas and Sianna vanish through the carpet of clouds, I notice how they've created a frame of lightning like the one Kaira made earlier. It looks like their version of a Velinis charm — a protective band of light, having the benefit of switching to attack mode if necessary.

"Wrap the lightning around you like a ribbon, then kneel and wait," Kaira instructs, showing us how it's done.

It's a simple trick to master, the five of us housed in our frames of lightning — ready for take off.

"You'll feel the competing forces in the skies as we drop," Kaira adds. "Trust your lightning frame to guide you in the right direction, and only fire at obvious threats."

"Like what?" Noah asks.

"A direct attack. You've got your Quivvens as additional protection, and a bond with the sky should you need it. Finally, Bloodseekers are very attractive and highly manipulative. They'll be waiting for our arrival so be prepared for their charm."

"Charming vampires," Noah comments. "Anything else?"

"Yes. The leaders of Kelph have a plan for Taeia, offering him a clear path to glory."

"No seven-year pilgrimage then," Conrad comments, remembering the passage all heirs of Devreack have to complete.

"And if they're successful?" Lucy asks.

"The realm of Devreack is weakened," I reply, making the connection between a volatile heir and the likely path he'll take. "If Taeia can't master magic in our world, he's hardly likely to accept seven more years of it *before* he gets what he wants."

"Sounds like it's time to meet some bad people?" Conrad adds, sensing we need to get moving. "Come on, let's see what these Bloodseekers are made of."

THE DESCENT TO KELPH IS MORE CO-ORDINATED THAN THE normal free fall Conrad and I take, involving sliding off our Williynx to tumble through the sky. Night Ranging keeps the fun of magical living alive, the tracking part free of danger most of the time.

The same can't be said for this form of free falling, our lightning frames connecting as we drop at speed. I notice how each frame connects in pairs ... a sort of romantic coupling before all our frames rotate as one, creating a defensive wall against potential threats.

I'm not sure what's out here or who's brave enough to wrestle with a king, even if he is losing his power. Anyone who can call lightning has got my vote in battle. I watch as Thylas stands proudly in his frame of lightning ... purple sparks flickering around him to signal the approach of a wizarding legend. The frame expands as Thylas and Sianna lift their arms, calling more lightning towards them until it seems like the sky is under their control.

I know better, of course, understanding the sky to be a comrade — like the sky urchins and Williynx in the S.P.M.A. If they can call lightning and control thunder, they've earned it ... not something Taeia's likely to do which makes me think of his likely path once more. What if he doesn't take on the seven-year pilgrimage, rejecting his rightful place on the throne of Devreack? What does Kelph have in store for him, and us?

The more I think about it, the less confident I am that this is going to end well. We could have chosen to stick with our Night Ranging roles, gliding through the skies and living it up in Rebel's Rest, but that life is dependent on what's going on up here.

It's not directly linked, but the last thing we need is a tyrant ruling the sky realms. I just hope Jacob's having some success getting through to Taeia, now he's been lumbered with training him in all things magical.

If anyone can get through to our lost boy, it's my brother but the memory of Taeia firing out in anger on The Hallowed Lawn stays with me, particularly the blind fury on his face ... the reason we're here ... to make sure our wonderland of magic isn't ruined by another deranged prince.

My first sight of Kelph is the sight of towers pointing to the sky: dark, Gothic towers rising through the clouds. Bridges dominate the landscape, connecting each section of the realm of pirates and Bloodseekers. Some of the bridges stand high in the sky, offering access to the towers while others hover lower, weaving through ramshackle buildings suspended in mid-air.

There's no-one visible as we pass the towers, lit up by windows and marked by flags. We've entered the realm of

Kelph and I've already got a bad feeling about it. My Quivven glows a soft blue beneath my skin, a reassuring sign that its protective powers remain in place.

To test this out, I close my eyes and smile as a panoramic vision floods in: the beauty of blind sight. There are plenty of people here, all right ... gathered in the dark towers and the ramshackle buildings.

"Why are they hiding?" Conrad asks as we descend together, connected even in an unknown land.

"Maybe it's a mark of respect," I reply, blinking through bloodshot eyes.

"Do you believe that?"

"Not really," I add with a smile.

I miss the touch of my boy wizard, but need to keep my mind on the job.

"I like your new look," Conrad adds. "It gives you an edge."

"I'm just happy I can still see," I joke as Noah gestures towards something above.

"We've got company," he states, looking to me for guidance.

He's never been this uncertain but, then again, how often do you see a thousand-strong army riding on fire towards you?

"It's tradition," Kaira adds, raising a hand to calm Noah's nerves. "A royal welcome."

"They don't look welcoming," Lucy adds, holding a lightning bolt in her hand just in case.

"Only time can kill a Winter King. Any alteration to this fate brings a brutal end."

"So, we're safe?"

"For now," Kaira replies, "so go easy with that bolt of lightning unless you want to start a war."

"Who are they?" I ask.

"The Axyiam — sky soldiers protecting the borders of Kelph. Trust me, it's good news they've arrived. They'll guide us from here which is when things heat up."

"Between Thylas and the leaders of Kelph?" I say.

"Yep, and the question of their plans for Taeia. They'll lie, of course, and it's our job to expose that lie before it's too late."

"What's wrong with their faces?" Noah asks.

"They work on scent — the reason they've got slits for eyes. It's not a good idea to show fear so trust Thylas and stay calm: no sudden moves."

Kaira's instruction helps us to relax a little, watching as the two thousand-strong lines arrive in a surge of fire, ready to show their respects to a king on his last quest.

12

PIRATES IN THE WINGS

As the two thousand-strong lines of sky soldiers reach us, I do my best not to look at their faces. Kaira's explained the reason they have slits for eyes but this doesn't make the sight less weird. They're a lot taller than your average wizard: an all-male army sent to escort us to wherever we're headed. The dress code in Kelph seems to be minimal, grey being the colour of choice.

The army riding on fire wear grey trousers and shirts without sleeves: shirts designed to reinforce their strength. They're definitely built for battle and there are no scars on their arms, meaning they're highly skilled or limited to a role as sky guides.

I get the feeling they've seen war and probably *like* it, flinching as they sniff, jerking at their ropes of fire as they do. They're feral, all right, but on their best behaviour so I keep Kaira's instruction in mind: no sudden moves.

Without a word, the two thousand-strong guides kneel out of respect to their royal visitor — the look on their faces signalling something else: resentment. They're the sky soldiers of Kelph, after all, not known for loyalty to others.

Casper and Kaira both described Kelph as a pirate economy, driven by leaders with a lust for power ... *not* the sky realm we need Taeia to end up in.

"To your leaders," Thylas says, gesturing for the silent army to stand, "I return in peace."

That gets me thinking ... Thylas's reference to peace suggesting a troubled relationship. A Winter King needs to fight his corner, and it's likely his main battles have been with the sky realm most keen to take his throne. Since it can't be taken by force — based on Kaira's comment that only time can kill a Winter King — no doubt this lot have thought up ways to weaken Thylas, accelerating his demise.

An arc of fire gets my attention ... the sight of the silent choir whipping their ropes of flames as if they're lashing the sky with contained fury.

"Follow the fire," Kaira says from within her frame of lightning.

As we fly through the sky within our frames of lightning, I wonder what we're headed towards ... the towers rising through the clouds or the ramshackle buildings linked by bridges floating in the sky. The answer comes quickly in the changing nature of the towers ... one sending out a streak of white light.

The light connects to each of our frames of lightning, pulling us forwards until we're moving as one towards the small windows decorating the tower ... windows that move out of their frames and float towards us until they're close enough to step through. Once the windows connect with our frames of lightning, we follow Thylas and Sianna — transported through glass to a chamber housing false allies.

The first thing I notice about the tower we appear in is the lack of floors. In fact, there's nothing inside at all except for the stone walls and windows. A silent group sit on stone thrones cut into the tower walls, waiting to see what a king has to offer them.

They're dressed in the same grey material as the sky soldiers who guided us here — the only difference is their grey has the glittering quality of Thylas' robes: a symbol of their superior position in a land of pirates.

At least they look more *human* than our silent guides ... normal features and familiar gestures ... the first one being a nod of welcome as their concrete thrones extend forward. It's an orchestrated move of power, closing in on us as we hover in mid-air, but the king in our company doesn't look bothered at all.

Things get more interesting when Thylas makes his own statement, using a simple charm to draw another window towards him, manipulating the glass to make a throne of his own. With a smile, I whisper 'Bildin', remembering that Society magic can be used with any material property.

Like Thylas, I draw a window towards me, deciding to decorate my glass throne with a tinge of blue. Kaira gives me a smile as I perch on my chair, watching as the others do the same. It's a lot better than swinging our legs in mid-air — not the statement you want to make in the company of a people who prey on weakness.

"You haven't lost your touch, Thylas," comes the first voice from the group surrounding us — the tallest woman of the group, managing to make the uniform grey of Kelph look elegant. "A throne fit for an ageing king."

"Ever the one to point at vulnerability, Uleya," Thylas responds, tapping his fingers to ignite sparks of light. Something tells me Thylas could blast every one of them into a thousand pieces — the reason they've given him a royal welcome.

The question is why he hasn't during his reign? I'm guessing it's something to do with the nature of being a king: the way power is wielded and the consequences of abusing it.

"I see you've brought company," the woman called Uleya adds. "Children from an earthly realm."

"Famous children," another voice adds ... stick-thin with rasping breath and an attitude to match. "The saviours of the S.P.M.A.," he adds with a tone of sarcasm, "coming to the aid of a royal legend."

"Nice to meet you," I say with a mocking smile. "It's nice being somewhere else for a while — not quite what I expected, but oh well ..."

"Arrogance is a fatal flaw, Guppy Grayling," the man adds, deciding to stand as he says it. "It may have helped in the battle that made you famous, but it will lead you into trouble in our world."

"Just offering the welcome I've been given," I reply, this time without the fake smile, "and I've been threatened plenty of times before."

"More of a friendly warning."

"We're not friends."

"Enough," Sianna states, standing to match the pose of power the figure annoying me has taken. "We are here to talk not argue, Goranev. The young magicians travelling with us are *our* guests; therefore, treat them as such or risk offending us all."

"No offence intended," Goranev adds, returning to his seat as Thylas stands from his, towering over the assembled presence of Kelph elite — ready to address the question of destiny and the boy on everyone's lips.

"As you are all aware, we are here to discuss time. I hope for reassurances from you whilst you seek certain conditions of your own. It is possible neither of us will be satisfied with the outcome, leading to continuing problems for us all. Time is against us so let's be brief and turn to the subject of my heir: Taeia Renn."

"The heir you see, Thylas," Uleya adds from her floating throne, "but you've admitted your visions are less stable than they once were."

"Taeia is my heir."

"An heir so unskilled in the art of magic? An heir so unstable and unaware of his path?"

"His lack of knowledge has been a conscious decision," Thylas adds, moving around the circle of floating thrones, his glittering, grey robes decorating the tower. "The sense of destiny will grow within him until it becomes an unbearable burden. At some point, he will choose to grasp it or abandon it: the critical point upon which our joint fates rest."

"You fear he'll reject his destiny," an ancient man states, standing with Thylas and offering a hand of welcome — the only genuine gesture I've seen so far.

"Yes, Orilin, which can only lead to death and destruction, because a wizard empty of remorse and tainted with royal blood will never rest easily."

"Yet, if he chooses another path like the one we offer to lost souls, we are not to blame, Thylas."

"If he chooses of his own free will, it is beyond anyone's power to stop him."

"You seem to doubt our intentions, Thylas," Uleya adds as I shift in my glass throne, sensing the tension growing in the air.

"Your history causes suspicion, Uleya: a history leading

to inevitable war should Taeia be persuaded away from his path of destiny."

"We've offered our reassurances many times, Thylas," Goranev adds in a less than persuasive tone.

"Yet I see something else," Thylas replies. "A co-ordinated attempt to align Taeia to Kelph. Such a disruption of a king's destiny will not be forgiven lightly. This is not a command from me but the *actuality* we live every day: an actuality many of you choose to ignore."

"We all have different actualities, Thylas," Uleya says, tapping her hands to send the stone thrones retreating to the tower walls. "The actuality of Kelph being the pursuit of influence."

"An obsession with power," Sianna adds in obvious frustration. "An obsession causing the suffering of many."

"Not everyone is destined for greatness," Uleya adds with a merciless smile, "so we will await the outcome of Taeia Renn's decision and continue our surveillance of him. We will not directly pursue him, but neither will we reject him if he chooses to divert from the fate you see for him. If this leads to war, it will not be a war of our making. We have our way and you have yours: a simple conclusion to our meeting."

"Adopting the moral high ground without the sincerity to match," Thylas adds as a look of fury forms on his face. "You forget that I see visions of many things, including visions of the future. I had hoped you would see sense in the end ... recognise the danger of diverting destiny ... but time is against us now so I must act in the way I see fit."

"You're a fading king, Thylas," Uleya adds. "Now isn't the time to test your power. Our sky soldiers will descend in seconds — think of your young comrades."

But Thylas isn't listening now ... his white eyes turning

on the Kelph elite who haven't provided the reassurances he hoped for. In fact, they've done little to hide their intentions without stating them outright. They're not going to bow to a king's command, something they're likely to regret.

"Thylas ... " comes the voice of the figure who offered a hand earlier.

There's something about the way he says it that makes me sense what's coming — the fury of a king with a point to prove. Thylas Renn might be fading but the sense of disrespect he feels is obvious ... a sense his influence is waning in the realms it's needed most in ... leading to a sudden statement of power that changes things.

A flash of light starts things ... lightning bolts directed at the tower windows before being redirected towards the stone thrones. The Kelph elite vanish before the blast is turned on them, leaving us to face the Kelph army that led us here, spiralling into a battle soon after. The rhythm of battle returns quickly, the ability to adapt as chaos swarms around us.

There are far less silent soldiers than on our arrival, making me feel this is a precursor to the real thing. They can't kill a Winter King, after all, and probably don't want to start a war between worlds by killing the rest of us, so battle formations are formed as the tower is swarmed with the Axyiam: servants to a cowardly crew who've vanished out of harm's way.

Kaira's done her own vanishing act, disappearing out of sight before reappearing lower down ... a sign the Disira charm works up here — good news when you're fighting in a crowded space.

"Connect before you vanish!" Kaira shouts to us all, firing out a blast of ice beneath us to dodge some unwelcome company.

Conrad, Lucy and Noah have already worked this out, connecting their charms to fragments flying through the air, or riding on the energy of friendly fire to dart out of danger. *Why* Thylas thought it would be a good idea to start an argument here is beyond me but here we are, getting an introduction to the dynamics in the sky.

"Just think, we could be in Rebel's Rest now!" Noah shouts as he spins in ribbons of fire, the Infernisi charm bursting into flames to send the enemy packing. "I thought we needed more lessons on advanced magic!"

"You're having a lesson now!" Lucy shouts back as Thylas lifts her to safety, avoiding the attentions of a Kelph soldier marked with blood.

"You'd think Thylas might have given us some warning!" Conrad adds as the tower explodes around us.

The next explosion is something else ... a roar of thunder rumbling above as rain pours down. Lightning follows soon afterwards ... used by Thylas to forge a path to safety. He looks like a god of the skies for the first time, clearly not intending fatal harm but more of a reminder his reign isn't over yet.

Commanding the skies surrounded by a web of lightning, he fires out blasts to send the enemy scattering, thunder roaring with his every attack.

"He doesn't look like a fading king to me!" Lucy says as the attack eases, leaving shattered thrones and fragments of glass spinning in the air around us.

"It's a warning shot to those watching in other realms," Sianna explains, sending strands of fire around her bare feet before adding, "and also our way back to Devreack. You know the ritual: no powder this time so either choose the glass or stone fragments as your path to the skies."

As the shattered tower shudders on the verge of collapse,

I utter 'Smekelin' to surround my feet in flames. Fragments of glass are my chosen pathway to the skies, concluding our introduction to battle in a realm vying for Taeia Renn's attention. It's obvious things are going to change up here soon, Thylas's sudden statement of intent a mark of things to come.

With the Axyiam retreating in perfect lines, I wonder when we'll return to Kelph and what we'll be met with. Something else is on my mind as I keep pace with the others: the enemy's blood spattered across my hands and arms, giving me the feeling we're not out of danger yet.

13

TURNING TIDES

I ride through the skies on my glass pathway, the Quivven glowing in my forearm. Fading or not, Thylas is clearly more powerful than any member of the Kelph elite who vanished as quickly as they appeared, leaving us with a very clear picture of their intentions. There's going to be a passing of the torch, all right, but any thoughts of it being a smooth transition has been thwarted.

Soon, we'll swap our roles as Night Rangers, taking our place on the sky towers overseeing the boundaries of the S.P.M.A. — surveillance points situated in Zilom, The Royisin Heights and The Goronoff Mountains, keeping an eye on Society members accepting invitations from the skies.

So, we're in a race against time, doing our best to keep an eye on Taeia before he makes his choice: to Devreack or elsewhere. If Jacob's made any progress in The Cendryll, he'll be able to offer some insight, but I'm not holding my breath.

Some people aren't cut out for magical living, and when the person in question has the potential to ruin a kingdom, it's a good idea to intervene before it's too late. It might be too late already, particularly if Taeia knows more than he's letting on. For all we know, he's just biding his time in The Cendryll, playing the role of fallen wizard seeking rehabilitation.

He isn't stupid enough to try anything around people more powerful than him, so he's probably sulking in the corner as Jacob teaches The Fateful Eight, secretly plotting his path to power.

"Guppy ... to your left," Kaira says, gesturing for me to veer away from new dangers.

We move as one with Thylas and Sianna speeding alongside us, choosing lightning as their sky path of choice.

"They pose no threat as long as we stay alive," Sianna explains as her greying hair whips in the wind. "Bloodseekers hovering in the channels they move in: an audience you should familiarise yourselves with."

The immaculately dressed onlookers stand in pockets of space, lining our path back to Devreack. None of them move out of formation as we pass, their striking looks at odds with their gruesome pastime.

"They don't look like killers," Noah adds, deciding to move a little closer.

"That's because they're not," Kaira reminds him. "They benefit from the kill, drinking the blood of the dead to build their strength."

"So, vampires without the killing bit."

"Something like that, Noah," Kaira adds, "although I wouldn't get too close because you might be invited in."

"Into where ...?"

"Wherever they choose to take you — most likely to a place where you'll come unstuck."

"Not very *friendly* up here, is it?" Noah comments before

swerving back into formation, offering a wave to the groups who look on, whispering to one another as we blast past them. They're regal, all right, but not giving off the same gentle power as the Society elders.

They seem out of time — as if they've lived this way for centuries, never adapting to a magical world that offers a less primitive way of life. Obviously, there's something about the taste of blood that's got them hooked: a drug they can't get enough of.

"Maybe we should give it a try," I say to the others as Sianna and Thylas storm towards the crackling sound of thunder. "You know, drink a bit of blood like Noah. Do you feel any stronger?" I ask, deciding a bit of teasing might lead to a race.

"Stronger than you any day, Grayling," Noah replies, banking left to cross my path.

I dart in the same direction, blowing a ball of fire in his direction ... just for the fun of it.

"Oi! Watch it! We've got company who wouldn't mind seeing me dead."

"Then you better get a move on," I reply, "before you're left behind."

That gets Noah moving, the sight of Thylas and Sianna vanishing increasing his sense of urgency.

"Some guides we've got," Lucy adds, blowing another ball of fire towards our silent onlookers: beautiful specimens with a scent for the dead. "You'd think they'd have mentioned we were heading into battle before we *got there*."

"It didn't look planned," Conrad comments, "as if Thylas hoped for a different outcome."

"It's his last stand," Kaira adds as she speeds alongside us, her hair lifting in the wind. "He knows his time's running out. It was a sign of vulnerability more than anything else."

"I doubt it's going to help," Lucy states as we race to catch Noah.

"It almost certainly won't," Kaira explains, "which is the reason we're here, hoping to stop a chasm forming."

"Will more people come up if things go *really* wrong?" I ask. "From the Society, I mean."

"Only a chosen few and only if absolutely necessary. Ultimately, we're guests here, Guppy, with no power beyond our skill and bravery. The blood bond we formed has aligned us to the skies, but *how* and *when* we connect to its full power is unknown."

"Well, let's hope we work it out soon before *that* lot get a taste for our blood," I add, riding alongside my friends towards the blasting sound of thunder ... thunder that spins in circles as we approach ... a circle for each of us ... returning us to the white fortress in the sky.

ONCE BACK ON THE CARPET OF CLOUDS, I DECIDE TO ASK MORE about our blood bond and the likely outcome of our fall out with the leaders of Kelph. With our Williynx re-appearing in the skies, I feel a sudden desire to fly off again — maybe to shake off the mild shock of battle or just for the sheer fun of it.

Conrad beats me to it though, asking about the blood bond, whether *we're* going to be drinking blood and the reason we ended up in a battle at all. After an uncomfortable silence, Thylas turns his white eyes on Conrad, offering the explanations we're all keen to hear.

"The bond we've formed will allow you to call on the sky's powers in time."

"Which is when?"

"When the skies of Devreack decide you're ready."

"But you called on the sky in Kelph?" Lucy queries.

"The sky is one essence in our world ... Devreack, Kelph, Whistluss ... its powers travel through them all. Once you've been blessed with a blood bond, you build trust over time. In your world, surveillance devices are used to test the intentions of witches and wizards. In ours, the sky dictates all things, including those worthy of its gifts and those destined for a downfall."

"Okay," Conrad says, seeming satisfied with the explanation. "Which means Taeia won't be able to draw on the sky's powers, assuming he turns out to be bad, that is."

"*Only* when he submits to darkness," Thylas explains, "and not until then. Even if he chooses to abandon his destiny, this alone will not alienate him from his connection to the sky. He remains a king in waiting until he does something to irrevocably change this."

"Like attack the throne he belongs on," I suggest.

"Precisely, Guppy. Many kings have abandoned their destiny over the centuries, using their powers in other realms and for other reasons. Royal ascension isn't a given, but a dutiful existence is. Without duty there is no purpose: the point at which your powers leave you."

"What about drinking blood?" Lucy asks "You got Noah to do it to stop the pain in his head. Are there other situations where we'll all need to drink it?"

"Many and none?" comes the reply that gets a puzzled look from us all. "In times of crisis, blood is always available as a remedy. Whether you choose to drink it or not is your choice."

"But it makes us stronger?" I prompt.

"If it's taken at the right time."

"Which is?"

"To remedy injury — not simply as an elixir of life."

"Which is how the Bloodseekers use it: as an elixir of life?"

"Yes, Lucy, meaning they live between life and death, caught in a cycle of their own making."

"And the battle you sort of threw us into?" Noah asks with growing confidence, sensing he's earned the right to ask the question.

"A taste of things to come, Noah; things which will involve you all soon enough."

"It just seemed a bit *random* since we were going there to talk."

"The talking's done," Sianna comments, placing a hand on Thylas' left arm — more out of concern than affection.

It's only when he staggers that I realise how weak he is, as if he'd mustered his last bit of energy in Kelph.

"The surrounding sky realms sense Thylas' fading state," Sianna continues. "The reason Uleya and the others had the confidence to challenge a king. This confidence will only grow, leading to an attempted coup, starting with the plot to gather Taeia Renn into a rival faction."

"Why not just let Taeia take the throne *then* work on getting on his good side?" I ask.

"Because the seven-year pilgrimage cleanses prospective heirs of all darkness in their soul. The moment Taeia takes the throne, his pilgrimage begins: an extended, hypnotic state only ended by its completion or failure."

"Failure being death," Conrad comments.

"Yes, which explains Taeia Renn's reluctance to take the throne when his time comes. A unskilled wizard will have little faith in himself, viewing a seven-year pilgrimage as certain death ... the reason the vision of the future is bleak ... a vision you must all see before it's too late."

"Thylas, you're not strong enough."

"The children must see, Sianna; the very reason they're here."

With his mind made up, Thylas raises his hand to the enormous, white Williynx protecting his kingdom. In seconds, he's whipped into the air on the back of his feathered companion, leading us to carry out the same manoeuvre, returning to the skies to learn the secrets hidden in a faltering kingdom.

14

A KING'S VISION

The reason for the impromptu sky ride soon becomes clear — a way of viewing the hundred pathways linked to the white fortress suspended in the sky. The Winter King's palace is colossal, the pathways making me think of tentacles attached to a royal hideout: tentacles that defend the kingdom with blistering attacks.

This almost certainly isn't the case but it's the thought that lingers as I glide on Laieya, happy to be in her company once more. Sky riding on our favourite Williynx is a more familiar feeling, particularly after darting through the sky on pathways of glass and ropes of fire.

In a lot of ways, riding a Williynx feels safer, mainly because they can shape shift and breath ice, something that might have come in handy in Kelph but that's another story. For now, all eyes are on Thylas as he rests on his enormous white Williynx: a rapidly fading king with a tale to tell.

"It looks like he's going to fall off," Conrad whispers as he glides closer, brushing my arm as he does so.

Romance has taken a back seat in the last few days, mainly because it's hard to be at ease in unfamiliar territory, so it's important to savour simple touches and the odd kiss when possible.

"Let's hope not," I reply, wondering if Conrad's just predicted Thylas' end: a final free fall through the carpet of clouds to an unknown resting place. Thankfully, this isn't the case and he stays on his white Williynx, his arms wrapped around his feathered companion's neck. As he raises his right hand again, the explanation of how the hundred pathways work begins.

"The royal fortress you see is both a blessing and a curse," Thylas begins, rubbing his white beard as he does so. "A blessing because it offers protection from all threats, and a curse because the pathways also offer visions of the future."

"How is that a curse?" I ask, rubbing specks of blood off my black, leather trousers. "Isn't it a good thing to be able to see the future?"

"Yes and no, Guppy," Thylas replies as Sianna glides close by, ready to intervene if he *does* topple to his death. "The ability to see the future burdens you with a particular responsibility."

"Like the Renns being water readers," Kaira comments, staying low on her Williynx as her blue, velvet waistcoat flaps in the wind. "I've heard the saying 'fate calls the Renns' a lot, helping me to understand why my dad and aunt have given so much to the Society. Maybe it's the same for you: blessed with a gift few have or maybe want."

"Wise words as always, Kaira," Thylas replies, offering a rare smile as he does. "I see you're less willing to accept the burden this time."

"I came back to help my family and friends, although how far I go will depend on a lot of things."

"Like what?" I ask, wondering if I should have asked the question, but if Kaira's checking out soon I'd rather know.

"On what we can actually achieve up here," Kaira replies, turning to me with those wise eyes. "Once Taeia's made his decision about where his future lies, we'll have either helped in diverting him away from temptation or failed in our duty. If we fail, we step into another battle — one I'm not sure I want to fight in."

"As you wish, Kaira," Thylas adds, his head dipping suddenly in a sign of decline. "However, before you make your decision a greater understanding of the power of The Winter King's fortress may help. The marks on the walls you've seen are spells written in ancient scripts: spells that protect the fortress and illuminate what stands at the end of each path.

The incantation to release these spells can only be understood by the rightful heir — never uttered in the presence of others; therefore, we have to use other means for you to glimpse the things that dominate my visions. In respect to your presence here, it is both critical and optional. We have no authority to ask other magical worlds to fight on our behalf."

"That's good to know," Noah comments as his fire-red Williynx spreads its wings, lifting him higher. "Not that I'm backing out, obviously, but if things go *spectacularly wrong* a return to Night Ranging might be a good idea.

"I'll help as long as you need me," I declare, wanting to make my position clear.

"Me too," Conrad echoes.

"And me," Lucy adds, flashing a look in Noah's direction. "I might be new to battle, but I'm definitely not backing out now. If our fate's in the skies, we may as well get used to it. No offence meant, Kaira."

"No offence taken," Kaira replies with another smile. "War takes its toll, that's all."

"Let's hope that can be avoided," Sianna adds, resting a hand on Thylas' trembling arm.

It's the clearest sign yet that this tower of a man is crumbling, using his final moments to explain the visions that are troubling him. "It's time," Thylas mutters to Sianna who nods in response, helping him to sit up before he does *exactly* what I feared, tumbling off his white Williynx into oblivion.

Well, at least that's what it looks like until we dart below the clouds to find him hovering on his back ... messiah like with arms outstretched as if he's waiting for the gates of heaven to appear.

"Is he dead?" Lucy whispers.

"He's moving between life and death, leaving us with a singular vision."

"Of what?" Noah prompts, holding on as his feathered companion shape-shifts into a smaller form.

Sianna doesn't respond, leaving us to wait in the skies of Devreack, hovering above the still figure of a king seemingly at rest, preparing for one final act. The majestic movement begins soon afterwards ... each of the hundred pathways connected to the white fortress stretching upwards ... attaching themselves to Thylas' floating figure. Each pathway moves *through* his body, generating shimmering visions of the past, present and future.

"Watch closely and avoid contact with the pathways," Sianna instructs, hovering in the air as the hundred pathways form a protective barrier around Thylas, almost as if they're accompanying him to his final resting place. As the intense visions of a hundred sky realms fill the Devreack sky, a Winter King's final act begins, his white eyes remaining closed as he pivots into an upright position.

He doesn't look or speak to any of us, suggesting he's unaware of our presence. With open hands, he utters an incantation in a strange language, calling the pathways towards him one after another, looking like a conductor leading an orchestra. I pat Laieya to keep her calm as we hover outside the floating cell of pathways, trying to make sense of the flickering visions of life in the sky realms.

As a gust of white air appears from Thylas' mouth, one of the pathways attaches itself to our fading king, wrapping him in its protective layer of light as if it's filling him with well-needed energy. Cocooned in the luminous pathway, Thylas' voice gets louder ... the strange incantations spoken at rapid speed as if time's against him.

The white air leaving his mouth floods the cocoon of light until letters can be seen — not letters I recognise but the marks covering the walls of his fortress. The letters swarm around him, moving like rivers in search of a particular moment until it appears: a vision of a boy wizard struggling with his destiny.

Taeia Renn flickers into life in the cocoon of light offering haunting visions. The first vision shows a young boy before his entrance into the S.P.M.A., walking alone through Founders' Quad as he pick-pockets passers-by. As the first image fades, the second forms of a Night Ranger storming through the skies at night *alone*, searching for something he senses is out there.

"He *knows*," Conrad whispers on the back of his turquoise Williynx. "He knows there's something in the skies."

"He senses it," Sianna replies. "The first sign of destiny

calling. The moment he sensed it marked the beginning of Thylas' end: a natural transition of power from a king to his heir."

"But he's never accessed the sky realms?" I ask, watching Taeia on his white Williynx, shouting in fury as he circles in the night sky, failing to uncover a secret he senses.

"He's never had the foresight or true alignment to the stars to access our world, although that will change soon. Thylas is fading rapidly but is convinced of the visions dominating his mind. Yes, they may be unstable as Uleya mentioned in Kelph, but I trust his visions and believe Taeia will find his way here. When he does, various sky channels open, hoping to tempt him away from his fate."

"I doubt it will take much," Lucy comments as a third vision appears ... of Taeia sitting on The Cendryll's skylight at night, fuelled by a familiar resentment as he fires charms into the air — charms that rattle through the buildings of Society Square.

"Looks like his training's going well," Noah jokes but his mistimed humour is ignored as Thylas lifts a trembling hand to the sky, guiding his cocoon of light higher as it stretches across the Devreack sky. What appears is the most definite sign of trouble brewing — of an heir storming towards Devreack on a black Williynx with vengeance in his eyes.

"You're confident of the visions?" Kaira asks Sianna as Thylas closes his eyes, the murmured incantations stopping as he does.

"The visions are unstable but, in my opinion, accurate."

"But they could be *inaccurate*?" Conrad challenges. "The leaders of Kelph didn't seem convinced."

"Because it gives them the excuse they need, arguing that their choices cannot be based on a fading king's visions.

Ultimately, it's the decision of each witch and wizard to believe what they choose. Put simply, if they are true the kingdom of Devreack is under threat: a kingdom operating as the axis to everything else."

"Well, if you ask me we've got a battle on our hands," Conrad comments as Thylas floats higher, his glittering, grey robes operating like sails as the pathway separates from him.

"It's close now," Sianna comments. "The skies are calling Thylas for the last time."

It's a different end to the ones I've seen before ... more peaceful as Thylas floats higher ... circling as he rises until his white Williynx appears in the sky beside him, offering a string of feathers in a gesture of farewell. The feathers rest over his eyes moments before he fades out of sight, making the transition from life to death in an unknown magical heaven.

I watch as the light stretching up from the hundred pathways also fades away, releasing its connection to a dead king — ready to form an affinity with his heir: an heir on a mission of destruction carried along on a bleak vision of black.

"What now?" Lucy asks as the sky rests in silence.

"We accept the stars have shifted and prepare accordingly," Sianna replies, "beginning with business at home."

A vacant look has taken over her, reminding me of her granddad's death after he released the final fragment of the Terrecet.

"Who's going to protect the empty fortress?" Noah asks.

"The soldiers who have done so for centuries."

"Williynx?"

"Williynx and the magic fused into the hundred pathways. There's no way in without express permission. Only the boy we're most concerned about has access now."

"Well, that's reassuring," Conrad adds as we turn away from the resting place of another legend, ready to fly back into familiar territory and a problem on the horizon.

15

SHIFTING STARS

The journey back to more familiar territory is similar to the way we arrived, but this time torrential rain forms a chariot controlled by our ropes of fire. We have our trusted Williynx with us, of course, but we've found a new form of sky riding so make the most of it.

Soon, we'll be back within the boundaries of the Society Sphere, touching down in Zilom where a mystical wizard's probably waiting for us. Aarav Khan's been an important adult guide so far, meaning it's likely he'll want to know how we got on in the sky realm, assuming he doesn't know already.

With the amount of surveillance devices in the S.P.M.A., it's surprising anything's hidden but secrets have their way of forming. Our fallout with the leaders of Kelph probably hasn't gone unnoticed, particularly by Society elders in magical faculties up and down the land.

I'm sure Casper and Philomeena have got a way of studying the stars — not to mention another scarred legend based in The Orium: Weyen Lyell. With Follygrins, Panorilums and Tabulals buzzing with information, we're likely to get a lot of attention once we touch down in the realm of suspended rain.

Zilom is our own sky realm of sorts, the multi-coloured strands of light lifting witches and wizards towards suspended platforms, glittering with light. Part of me is looking forward to relaxing in Zilom before our return to The Cendryll, swinging with Conrad as we look over the fountain of suspended rain.

Whether we'll have time to do this isn't up to me, but I imagine Lucy and Noah could do with some alone time. Also, Kaira has that absent look on her face, suggesting a bit of peace and quiet won't do her any harm. Aarav's nowhere to be seen when we touch down, meaning we have the alone time I hoped for.

Kaira's the first to create a platform in the evening sky, using the Bildin charm and a handful of purple raindrops to build a glittering bridge.

"See you on the other side," she offers with a smile, suggesting she's used Zilom's unique Periums before.

There's no point trying to persuade Kaira otherwise; she looks tired and aware she's in the company of two couples. I want her to know she's still a central part of life, but I also understand the dynamic's different between us now — me balancing Society life and alone time with Conrad while Kaira moves between worlds alone: her father's daughter in every respect.

Wise, distant and burdened in the same way her dad and aunt are, Kaira waves goodbye as she walks along the purple bridge lighting up the Zilom sky: a friend with a choice to make.

I've already made up my mind, choosing to return to the sky realms and fight if necessary. It might not come to that, but it's hard to forget the image of Taeia roaring towards

Devreack on the back of a black Williynx. I didn't even know black Williynx existed although white ones are fairly rare too.

"Well, we're going to make a bridge of our own," Lucy says, uttering 'Bildin' as she reaches for a handful of coloured raindrops.

I get the feeling Lucy wants to hang out in Zilom as well, maybe because she's angry with Noah's suggestion he might back out of helping in the skies, or just because she wants to feel the comfort of familiarity again. It's easy to forget Lucy and Noah haven't travelled much beyond well-known places, looking for fun or shifty witches and wizards.

It's a *big* jump to a battle in the skies so I go along with Lucy's wishes, helping her build a swing bridge as Conrad and Noah stand on a circular platform of light. Romance is on hold while we process recent events, including Kaira's next steps: a friend who releases a Spintz charm in a sign she's returning home.

I still imagine home as The Cendryll for Kaira. It's the place where everything started, after all, and the place I now call home. Hopefully, when we've sorted things out in the sky I can catch up with Kaira, reforming the unique bond I've got with her. Maybe I'm struggling to accept my friend has moved on, or maybe I need to make more of an effort now she's back.

There's hardly been time to do either, so I decide to make this a priority as soon as I can. First though, I've got my boy wizard and Night Ranger comrades to consider, so I join Lucy on her yellow bridge decorating the sky, offering the comfort she seems to need.

As Conrad and Noah jump off their circular stage, generating other circles of light to fall through — a way of keeping their minds off things, maybe — I check in with

Lucy who's got the look of someone on the verge of a big decision. She might have already said she'd fight if necessary, but the closer we get to that point in time the harder it's going to be for her. I know how it feels to put your life on the line at a young age, and the scars it leaves.

"You'd think they've just come back from a Night Ranging mission, the way they're fooling around," Lucy comments as Conrad and Noah spin more hoops of light into existence, creating a joyride in the Zilom sky as Lucy ponders her fate.

"It's their way of dealing with things, maybe," I suggest, holding out my hand to catch a handful of colourful raindrops.

I use the raindrops to wash away the specks of blood on my forearms: a reminder of the minor battle in Kelph and the Bloodseekers who lined the skies, watching our journey home. I wonder how long it will be before we see the ugly side of the Bloodseekers — their striking looks hiding a lust for death.

"You already think Taeia's chosen his path," Lucy adds, adjusting the fringe of her cropped, black hair: the pixie girl with a warrior spirit.

"Don't you?"

"Well, it looks that way unless Thylas was so weak he couldn't control his visions."

"I think Thylas held on for us," I say, swinging my legs over the shimmering bridge as Conrad and Noah whizz past.

"A passing of the torch," Lucy adds with a smile.

"Sort of, yes. Thylas knew he was dying and maybe also knew any battle would involve young witches and wizards again."

"So we don't have a choice?"

"We *always* have a choice, Lucy."

"And you'll always choose to fight?"

"Maybe not," I reply, "but as long as I'm a Night Ranger, I'll step up if needed."

"Conrad always said you were fearless."

"Stupid more like it," I counter which gets a laugh from Lucy: a laugh that releases tears.

"It's so *overwhelming*," she whispers, blushing with embarrassment as she wipes her tears away. "Fighting to protect a kingdom, watching a king die and trying to stop a comrade from wreaking havoc."

"Trust me, I know the feeling," I say, deciding we need a bit a fun of our own, "but there's always magic to cheer us up."

With that, I fire a Spintz charm into the evening sky ... one after another until we've got an arc of multi-coloured light above us. I wait for Lucy to catch on, smiling when she uses the Bildin charm to create our mode of transport home: a small sailing boat hovering nearby.

"After you, madam," I say in a strange accent which gets another laugh. "We have a decent wind so should reach our destination in good time."

"Why, thank you," Lucy replies, going along with the performance as she adds an umbrella, holding it above her head as if she expects a storm.

There's no storm brewing — just the pretty, colourful raindrops hanging around us like a chandelier of light. We've decided not to use the suspended rain to explore more of Zilom but, instead, sail through our archway of light to return to more familiar territory.

"Oi! What about us?" Noah calls out as he and Conrad appear above us.

"All aboard!" I shout, using the Acousi charm to blast out the sound of a horn.

Lucy's relaxing finally, joining in as we blast the sound of a cruise ship exiting its harbour.

Conrad and Noah land in the boat as we enter the archway of light, Conrad putting an arm around my waist as we ease into darkness.

"I thought you were leaving without me," he says with *that* smile.

"You seemed to be enjoying yourself."

"Speaking of enjoying ourselves ..."

"I'm a busy girl these days."

"Too busy for your boy wizard...?"

"That depends on what tricks you've got up your sleeve."

I leave Conrad to think about a different sort of magic, watching as Lucy rests her head on Noah's shoulder: a girl in need of reassurance and a loving touch before she makes the decision of a lifetime.

KAIRA'S SITTING IN THE SEATING STATION WHEN WE RETURN, the four of us falling through The Cendryll's skylight into a magical faculty resting in darkness. Surprisingly, Kaira's alone with only her Follygrin for company: a way of keeping her close to her loved ones. We head over to join her, walking across the S.P.M.A. logo dominating the marble floor. It always feels good to return here: a reminder of how lucky I am to have found such a place.

Casper, Philomeena and Jacob are nowhere to be seen, reinforcing the feeling we have to make our own way in a new crisis. Not a crisis of our making or one that directly threatens our magical universe — more a question of the limits of duty. It's the question we'll all have to answer at some point, although I doubt any of us are going to pull out now. Magic gets a *hold* of you after a while, seeping into your bones and dreams.

Of course, we could leave Sianna to it, deciding Night Ranging is all the trouble we need, but there's the guilt to consider. In the end, Thylas called on us to help so it probably won't go down well if we decide to hang out in Rebel's Rest with trouble brewing. I sit alongside Kaira, studying the moving illustrations in her Follygrin.

She's checking on her dad and aunt who've returned to 12 Spyndall Street: their above-ground house. They can hardly be blamed for wanting time out of all things magical, although I'm surprised they've chosen this point to get some distance.

"I know that look on my dad's face," Kaira says, offering me a smile as I budge up alongside her.

"He looks worried," Conrad says, sitting on the other side of Kaira. "You don't think ..."

"Think he's considering joining us in the sky realms," Kaira interrupts. "Probably, but I doubt he will; he isn't strong enough to survive another battle."

"Will that stop him going?" Lucy asks, standing with Noah in the centre of The Seating Station.

"I hope so," Kaira adds absently. "My dad's given enough to protect the S.P.M.A. My aunt too. If it's anyone's turn, it's ours."

"So, you're hanging around for a while?" I ask.

"If it keeps you out of trouble, I might as well," Kaira jokes, taking off her velvet jacket to reveal the faint scars on her arms.

We share the marks of war and memories of friendship, and the idea of Kaira sticking around makes everything seem better. I catch Lucy and Noah glancing at Kaira's scars, surprised at the marks covering her arms.

"Do they bother you?" Lucy asks. "The scars, I mean."

Kaira looks up at Lucy with one of those wise smiles. "They used to but not anymore. In a weird way they're proof that *all of this* is real. You'd be surprised how many times I've doubted that fact."

"But you've travelled *everywhere*," Noah adds, rubbing his arms as if he senses future scars.

"A lot of places, yes, and hopefully a lot more. That doesn't mean the doubt goes away, particularly when I go above ground."

"And is that why you all fought in the last war?" Lucy adds, beginning to understand *how* we could have made such a sacrifice.

"For me, yes," Kaira replies, rubbing the scars on her golden-brown skin. "I mean, what would *you* give to protect all of this?"

"Anything," Lucy replies.

"Then you've got your answer. In the end, it's a choice between endless magic or endless boredom."

I smile at this remark, mainly because I feel exactly the same way: a point I reinforce by adding. "Imagine going back to *school* every day, or taking a *bus* to get somewhere."

"I think I'd throw up and cry," Noah comments, acting as if he's going to vomit now.

It's the comic moment we all need to forget about the drama in the skies for a while — a comment that draws a laugh from us all. Our laughter fades at the sight of movement beyond The Cendryll's skylight ... sparks of light followed by a shadow looming.

It doesn't take a genius to work out who's sat up there, brooding and alone, although it looks like our troubled wizard's got company. Kaira's onto it straightaway, opening her Follygrin and waiting for the words 'Ask and you will Find' to appear.

"Taeia Renn," she whispers, leaning closer as a moving illustration forms.

The image is similar to the one Thylas painted for us in his last moments ... of Taeia firing out charms into the sky, but this time he's not alone ... the outline of my brother keeping him company.

"Do you think Jacob's getting through to him?" Conrad asks.

"If anyone can, Jacob will," I reply, rubbing the edge of the Follygrin to magnify the image before adding, "Is Taeia crying?"

"Looks like it," Noah adds, kneeling to get a closer look.

"So, maybe Jacob *is* getting through to him," Lucy comments as Taeia puts his head in his hands.

"The fact he's struggling could turn out be a good thing," Kaira says, handing me the Follygrin as she stands and walks to the centre of the marble floor, positioning herself directly under the skylight. "It means the darkness hasn't taken hold yet."

"So, we've got a chance of persuading him to take the right path," I say, joining Kaira.

With a nod, my friend adds, "I had a grandfather who everybody despised until he turned out to be our saviour. Taeia's hasn't got my grandfather's gifts, but he hasn't proven himself to be evil yet, either ... so we give him time."

"What does the water say, Kaira?" Conrad asks, prompting Kaira to use her family's powers as water readers.

"It's why my dad and aunt have gone above-ground, to use a Nivrium in private."

"And...?" I ask.

“It looks like the stars are shifting in the sky realms ... towards the boy wizard up there with Jacob ... caught in a storm of fate and temptation.”

“So, it’s a waiting game,” Lucy states as the five of us stand together, looking up at the boy with destiny in his grasp.

16

JACOB'S BURDEN

We go our separate ways after watching Jacob do his best to comfort Taeia — the two of them sitting on top of The Cendryll's skylight like long-lost friends. They're definitely not friends but Jacob's as kind as they come, meaning we're still in with a shot of turning Taeia away from oblivion.

Conrad finds a few tricks up his sleeve after sneaking into my room in the early hours. It's not 'the done thing', allowing underage witches and wizards to spend the night together, meaning we're treading a thin line between passion and trouble.

There needs to be time for young love, even in the midst of a new madness, so we do our best to make the most of the night, trying to keep our mind off other things. The other things in question include Jacob's progress with Taeia, Kaira's decision to stay and protect the sky realms and whether Lucy and Noah are ready for what's awaiting us.

After working on our own recipe of love, we sit opposite each other on my bed, discussing our likely futures.

"How long before Taeia finds his way through?" Conrad asks, referring to the sky realms.

He's dressed in just his jeans, leaving his white T-shirt on the bed to cool off. I'm not complaining, eyeing his lean torso and scar running across his body. It's the scar that almost killed him and the one he's most proud of. I think it makes him look sexier which he doesn't disagree with.

"Not long now Thylas has gone," I reply, sitting under the bedcovers and enjoying a bit of slow time. "We need to catch up with Jacob before his lessons start. Hopefully, he's got somewhere with Taeia."

"I doubt it," Conrad adds, whispering 'Exhibius' to reveal the map on my ceiling.

It's a map of all the places we've been to, covering Society Square and beyond. There's another universe to add now or, at least, a fraction of it ... Devreack and Kelph ... two sky realms in a battle for a young wizard's powers. The good news is Taeia hasn't discovered his powers yet, meaning we've still got time to work out what's eating away at him.

From the mess he was in earlier, sitting alongside Jacob on top of The Cendryll's skylight, it looks like a simple battle between light and dark impulses raging in him, but things are rarely simple in the S.P.M.A. so the best thing to do is keep watch until we know more.

As Conrad reaches towards the ceiling, adding The Winter King's fortress to the moving map of wonders, I think about Kaira returning to her above-ground home in 12 Spyndall Street, wanting to spend time with her dad and aunt before another journey begins.

She's back but in a different space — part of our group but separate at the same time. Maybe it's a fear of losing more loved ones that makes her keep her distance, or maybe it's the uneasy relationship she has with Society duty. Either way, I've got to leave my friend to it and accept things as they are, beginning with helping Conrad complete the addition to the map.

It's hard to stay focused with his lean, scarred torso so close but I do my best, resisting the temptation to pull him down onto the bed. As I use the Canvia charm to add the massive, white Williynx onto the fortress in Devreack, I feel the brush of Conrad's hand on my skin. It's a touch I've missed and want more of, pushing my body into his until the kiss I'm looking for comes.

"Shame we can't hide out here for a while," Conrad whispers with a smile. "You now, leave the Bloodseekers to take care of Taeia."

"Unless he becomes one himself," I reply, getting a strange look from Conrad. "Well, why not? If he's going to turn his back on a kingdom, who's to say what happens next."

"Spending a life tracking dead people," Conrad adds with a shrug. "I suppose it's better than killing everyone in sight."

"That's a bit dramatic."

"I'm the dramatic type."

"You're telling me."

"In fact, I feel a song coming on."

"Oh, God," I reply, pinching him to stop him booming out a tune and getting us into trouble.

"Okay, a dance instead?" Conrad offers, holding out his arms as he moves on the edge of the bed, dancing to a tune in his head.

I join in for the fun of it, taking his hands and moving to his rhythm, hoping we can stay like this until the morning light streams in.

Jacob wakes us up, knocking on the door of my bedroom which he rarely does: a sign he's learned something or is more worried than before. As Conrad's keeping me company, I creak the bedroom door open, peering at my brother through tired eyes.

"Another late night?" Jacob asks, catching a glimpse of Conrad hiding under the bed sheets. "I haven't got long so I'll wait in the dining room."

He doesn't seem bothered by Conrad's presence, clearly keener to fill us in on what's happened since we've been away. With our romantic evening over, we snap into action, getting showered and dressed — ready for an update from a brother with his own magical gifts.

Jacob's got a strange affinity with Society creatures, like the way he stopped Oweyna ripping Taeia's head off on The Hallowed Lawn. Oweyna's the first white Williynx I saw, wondering why she'd chosen Taeia for a companion. Winter Kings are decorated in white, I now know, the reason Taeia had the luck to ride on Oweyna. *That's* changed, obviously, and if Thylas's final vision is accurate, our lost boy will be riding on a black Williynx soon enough.

I haven't got my head around the idea of a black Williynx yet, confused by the idea completely. Williynx originate from Gilweean, after all — a realm of peace and beauty — so how does a *black* Williynx fit into this? I park the thought for now, sorting my hair and black outfit before stepping into the dining room, finding Jacob standing over a tower of toast: some things never change.

"Hungry?" I joke, walking over to give my brother a hug.

He's still critical in my life, keeping his own distance as I grow up: the big brother who's always there when I need him.

"Starving," he replies, using the Magneia charm to spin the toast towards him. "Breaking Society rules again?"

"You know me."

"The Society elders wouldn't approve."

"An Invisilis charm takes care of that," I reply with a smile, biting into a piece of toast.

"Young love," Jacob comments, raising his eyebrows.

"How's your love life?"

"Non existent."

"Scared of getting your heart broken?"

"Scared of getting blown up by my students, more like it."

"Even more reason to have some fun and loving."

"Jacob's getting some fun and loving...?" Conrad says, joining in on the teasing as he appears out of the bedroom, his copper blonde hair dripping wet.

"I was actually talking about yours."

"Weird," Conrad replies, catching the toast Jacob sends his way.

"Just a brother's concern."

"Well, Guppy's treating me very well," Conrad quips, stuffing the toast in his mouth.

"Moving away from the topic of love for a minute, it looks like things are accelerating in the sky realms."

"You could say that," I reply. "Thylas has gone and Taeia's going off the rails. We saw him with you last night, crying on top of The Cendryll."

"He's troubled, all right."

"What are the chances he stays on the right path?" Conrad asks, sitting opposite Jacob at the dining table.

"Taking his place as The Winter King and starting his seven-year pilgrimage?"

"Slim," Jacob states, a familiar shadow of concern crossing his face. "He resents everything we're doing for him — even my intervention on The Hallowed Lawn. It's like he's got no ability to appreciate anything."

"How long?" I ask.

"That depends on how quickly he learns to read the stars," Jacob adds. "The reason he's been sitting on top of The Cendryll at night."

That shakes me out of my sleepy state. "How could he learn to read the stars?"

"He's the heir to the kingdom in the stars," Jacob replies matter-of-factly. "A wizard with no special gifts in our magical universe, born with the ability to sense the one realm he's destined to rule."

"So, he gets more powerful now Thylas has gone?" Conrad queries.

"Yep, and it won't be long before he finds his powers."

"And when he does?"

Jacob stands, collecting the empty plate from the table. "When he does the stars will align, forming into the map hidden in the skies. From there, Taeia will have the choice we all know is waiting for him, but you need to see something before that happens."

"What's that?" I ask.

"The influence he's having over the other students."

"Leading them astray?"

"More than that. Come on, lessons start soon. You can see for yourself."

With the toast eaten and news of Taeia's search in the stars, we leave my bedroom and head across The Floating Floor — the walkway of illusory water hiding the Phiadal below. It's the place where all bovies are kept: artefacts with unknown magical properties.

The Phiadal started the race to find The Terrecet along with my mum's demise: a mum I need to see soon before things take off up above.

Spiral Way takes us to this morning's lesson — a spinning structure taking those keen on strange travel towards their destination. It's another ride into the air although limited to the space hidden behind an unremarkable door.

I remember the first time I saw it, walking with Kaira's aunt to get Jacob out of his 'cell' cataloguing charms. Well, not a cell but not a hotel, either, an example of how harsh my mum could be in her day.

Those days are long gone, mum's name no longer mentioned and Jacob rising to the status of teacher, about to show us The Fateful Eight's progress and how Taeia's arrival has affected them. With Lucy and Noah returning to The Leverin — the faculty for penchants — Jacob, Conrad and I step off the swirling structure of Spiral Way.

We offer nods of recognition to familiar faces as we reach our destination. There's no trip to The Hallowed Lawn on the cards this morning, suggesting there's no game of Rucklz planned — probably a good thing considering it's what triggered Taeia's fury.

"Any clues on what to look for?" I ask my brother.

"Silent influence," Jacob replies, offering no more than that.

"In a bad way, I imagine."

"Hard to say because the students' behaviour hasn't changed, but *something* has."

"Like what?" Conrad queries.

"That's the mystery," Jacob replies, "and something we need to solve before Taeia finds a path to the skies."

"Because he'll use it up there, whatever power he's got?"

"Yep."

"Well, I'm going to Rebel's Rest when we're done here," I say. "Catch up with some friends just in case I get on the wrong side of some Bloodseekers."

"You've dealt with a lot worse than Bloodseekers, Guppy," Jacob replies, "and that's not an image I need right now."

"Sorry ... just putting it out there."

"Well, let's hope we *can* avoid a battle in the skies. Here we go, my little teaching sanctuary: get ready for a show."

17

A TROUBLED HEIR

The room we enter is one I remember — the place I first learnt how to use a Cympgus with Kaira's aunt. It's Philomeena Renn's old hideout on the fifth floor where Quij flutter in through the small holes in the stonework. Another cool thing about the room is the way the holes let in the light beaming in from The Cendryll's skylight, almost within touching distance if you could magically make the stone walls disappear.

Magic is the reason we're here, saying our hellos to The Fateful Eight who we last saw battling it out on The Hallowed Lawn. They all seem to have grown except for Olin Zucklewick who sits on one of the windowsills, looking out over Founders' Quad. Olin makes up for his shortcomings in size with a sharp mind: a student likely to pass the final assessment when it comes.

It's a way of separating those destined for a life in a magical universe, sending the others back to the above-ground world with modified memories courtesy of the Removilis charm. The other student in question sits on the windowsill alongside Odin — Taeia Renn — wizard on the path to a kingdom or destruction.

I try to pick up on the 'silent influence' Taeia has over the younger students — Jacob's only explanation of the way the energy's changed since his arrival. He's still got the arrogant look and bitter smile, deciding not to throw out his usual put down on our arrival.

In some ways, Taeia's got all the marks of royalty. He's a Renn for one, handsome and regal in the way of all Renns, but there are two missing ingredients: humility and magical ability. He hasn't got the gifts expected of a Renn — or a king for that matter — and hasn't been humbled by his recent humiliation on The Hallowed Lawn.

His teacher was his saviour then, my brother who claps his hands to stop the morning chatter. With the beautiful, luminous Quij fluttering in and out of the room, Jacob takes out a Vaspyl to start the morning's lesson.

"You were all given Vaspyls last week and your homework was to practice using them, mainly for defence. Today, we're looking at how we can use them for shelter and then attack."

"Yes!" Ethan Lyell shouts, another Renn in the mix, sharing Taeia's good looks without the arrogance or bitterness. Ethan's been humbled in the last few weeks, realising he's falling behind in assessments. The difference being he hasn't got into a mood about it, apparently training day and night to improve.

"Create your desks and get ready," Jacob adds, pointing to the ceiling with his steel cane as he does. Transforming his piece of morphing steel into a cane adds to his authority, the Society tie marking him as a teacher loosened as usual.

"Is Kaira coming to the lesson today?" Tilly Flint asks,

concentrating on the ceiling where she's creating a desk and chair, courtesy of the Bildin charm.

"Not today," I say, watching as the other students create their own desks of light and energy, laughing as they do.

"Are they sitting upside down on the ceiling for a reason?" Conrad asks, wiping the water running down the back of his neck.

Jacob's early arrival didn't give us a lot of time to get ready, making us seem a bit dishevelled: not the ideal look for a Night Ranger.

"We're going to have steel objects flying around the room in a while," Jacob replies, adding,"Feel free to stay put and duck out of the way though."

"We'll sit on the windowsill when Taeia decides to move," I say, eyeing the shifty wizard with a victim complex.

"He's doing his usual thing," Jacob adds, "waiting for me to notice him before he sulks into position."

"This silent influence thing you mentioned," Conrad adds. "Can you give us *anything* to go on?"

"You'll see what I mean when the lesson starts," Jacob replies, clapping his hands for Taeia to get a move on which our lost boy does, wearing his usual smirk of disdain.

You'd think he'd be more grateful to Jacob for saving his life but, then again, some people aren't grateful for anything, making me wonder if we're dealing with a sociopathic wizard ... the last thing I need after being woken up so early.

"I don't suppose you could magic us some coffee," I say to Jacob who doesn't bite. He's clearly not in the mood for humour this morning, so Conrad and I take our place on the windowsill, glancing down at the morning shoppers on Founders' Quad.

"So," Jacob begins, looking up at his students sitting on

their upside down desks on the ceiling. "I hope we're all comfortable."

A ripple of laughter carries through the room, except for Taeia who sits with his hands on his head, trying his best to look unimpressed.

The Vaspyl was made by a famous Follygrin who, after days without sleep trying to perfect the artefact, shouted 'I need my bed!' and the morphing steel sprung to life, giving him just that.

"Can I go back to bed now," Ava Blin asks, her tall legs stretching under the luminous desk.

"And miss out on training for an important assessment," Jacob counters. "Be my guest, Ava."

She doesn't take my brother up on this offer, grimacing at her misplaced humour.

"We've had the pleasure of Conrad and Guppy's company before, but they're not here to help today."

"Ohhhh," comes the collective sigh from the class.

"They're here as onlookers."

"What's the point of that?" Roan Khan adds, a thinner, more uptight version of his cousin, Noah.

"Because they'll be helping me make the final cut."

That shuts Roan up — the thought of a trio choosing who survives and who leaves more daunting than just his teacher. Maybe it's because he seems intimidated by me, although I'm not sure why. The all-black attire helps with my Fire Witch reputation, but I'm hardly glaring and barking orders at anyone.

Either way, this revelation gets the *full* attention of the class, including Taeia who moves his hands away from his face, flicking his Vaspyl into the air to create a spinning top.

"We're going to see how you get on with making shelters from morphing steel," Jacob says, opening his hand to call a flurry of Quij to him. Once the delicate creatures are in the palm of his hand, their wings buzzing softly, Jacob closes his eyes ... a silent request turning the Quij blood red as they rest around the perimeter of the ceiling.

"That doesn't look good," whispers the ever-competitive Katie Flint, turning her Vaspyl into a blade as if she's worried the transformed Quij are about to attack.

Generally speaking, blood red Quij are a *very* bad sign but it's obvious Jacob's doing this to keep the class on edge, wanting them wound tightly to simulate a scene of conflict. As lucky as we are to live in a peaceful magical world once more, you never know what's around the corner: the current problems in the sky realms a perfect example of this.

"Do they bite?" Tom Koll asks — the most insecure of the group, mainly because of his family name: a name linked to an evil wizard no one likes to talk about.

"Only if you don't pay attention," Conrad replies from our position on the windowsill, ready to study progress and a mysterious silent influence. Whatever influence Jacob's picked up on is lost on me. Yes, Taeia's silent but what can be read into that?

"He's whispering to himself," Conrad says, gesturing to Taeia. "Look, he's using things to guard his mouth ... his hands and now the spinning top he's made from his Vaspyl."

"Some sort of incantation?" I ask. "The way he's influencing the others."

"Could be but, more importantly, where has he learnt to do it?"

"Must be spending a lot of time in The Pancithon: the library that helped us find out important stuff."

"Taeia? In the library?" Conrad challenges, shaking his head. "Not a chance. There must be someone else teaching him things ... *outside* of normal school hours."

"We should use a Follygrin to keep track of him."

"Or, even better, follow him when he's sneaking about at night and see who's company he's keeping."

"Deal," I say as the first student eases down from the ceiling, her chair of pink light stretching down until she pivots, landing on her feet: Leah Creswell at the ready.

"She looks like she *always* does her homework," Conrad whisper, probably referring to Leah's bookish appearance.

"Vaspyl at the ready, Leah," Jacob instructs, lifting his cane as he does so. "Remember, I'll use my cane to send something your way — not dangerous in any way but designed to force you into retreat. The shelter you build with your Vaspyl *must* be fit to protect you from whatever I send your way: understood?"

Leah nods, crouching with an intense look on her face. She means business, all right, so it's time to see who's been doing their homework. With a flick of his cane, Jacob releases a cloud that hovers over Leah, making her hesitant ... unsure whether to build the shelter straight away or wait for a downpour. No rain falls from the cloud, though, leaving Conrad and I to share a puzzled look.

"I hope he doesn't drag this out because I want to head out to Society Square," Conrad comments, "work on my dance routine before we're dragged back up *there*."

"What's with you and dancing all of a sudden?" I ask.

"I just need to move my dancing feet."

"Two left feet, you mean."

"You love my swinging hips."

"Oh, God," I add, trying not to laugh before Jacob flicks his steel cane again, causing the cloud to fill the room, limiting our vision and putting Leah in a difficult spot.

"What am I supposed to be sheltering against?" she shouts in frustration, but Jacob doesn't answer. Instead he closes his eyes before looking up at the ceiling, murmuring something like Taeia's been ... only Jacob's got a visible weapon resting on the periphery of the ceiling ... a blood-red army of Quij who buzz down in a swirling line, easing into the mist made by the cloud until Leah's scream fills the room.

A smash of metal follows — first a cage with Leah inside, morphing quickly into a steel drum to stop the Quij swarming.

"I thought you said it wouldn't be dangerous?" the small figure of Olin Zucklewick shouts down from his suspended position on the ceiling.

"*Simulating* danger, Olin," Jacob replies, flicking his cane to send the blood-red Quij in Olin's direction.

The smallest of the students, Olin always reacts the quickest, never fretting and able to adapt with imaginative defences. His Vaspyl morphs into multiple steel cases, a perfect shape to cover the lamps in the room, sending us into darkness. Trusting the Quij are only threatening attack, Olin also knows the tiny, luminous creatures rest once the light dies in The Cendryll.

He's worked out the unique creatures decorating our magical faculty will head for the only natural light on offer, streaming through the holes in the stone walls and back to delivering books. Olin's fast thinking gets a round of applause from the others, flinching as the Quij flutter past, returning to their delicate, colourful forms.

"Why don't you make it dangerous to *really* test us out?" comes the voice of Taeia who's been whispering to himself the whole time. What *is* he up to? I wonder as his chair stretches down towards the floor — not that Jacob's invited him down.

"Because you don't seem to deal with danger well, Taeia,

that's why?" Jacob replies, stepping forward to make his presence felt. "After all, you needed rescuing the last time you were in real danger."

"I didn't ask you for help."

"Your tears gave you away ... when you were hiding out in the trading lane."

"Well, why don't we see who needs help this time?" Taeia adds, taking a step closer to Jacob before he feels something pulling at his throat: a sign he's *definitely* not in control.

Jacob's using his steel cane as a magnet, dragging Taeia closer to him to establish who's in charge.

"I'm not going to make it here anyway," Taeia croaks, placing a hand over his throbbing throat, "so why don't we put an end to this so I can fail with a bang."

"*I'll* decide if you fail and whether you stay here."

"Is that what you think, Jacob? That you can *make* me stay? I can walk out into the above-ground world now and never come back."

"Then you really are as blind as you seem, Taeia, because no witch or wizard just walks out without consequence."

"Wiping my memory. *Do it* because I *don't belong here*, do I? *They* know because I couldn't even compete in a game of *Rucklz*, for God's sake!"

"The moment you lost your head," Jacob adds with a look of warning. "It would be unwise to embarrass yourself again, particularly when our young students are looking on."

"*I want you to fail me.*"

"Because you fear that's what you are," I say, deciding to call Taeia out for what he is: a coward.

"Who asked you, Grayling?"

"I don't need permission to speak, Taeia. I've done more to protect the Society than you ever will."

"Maybe, but I know why you're really here."

"Why's that?" Conrad asks, standing with me as we move towards Jacob.

"To *spy* on me. Why would you waste your time *watching a lesson* when you could be out there in the skies?"

"Well, there's not much to see apart from your usual sulking and whining," Conrad adds, "so why don't you just *get on with* the lesson instead of making another scene? If you do fail, so what? Everybody fails, but you've never even *tried* to belong here although you desperately want to."

A bitter laugh draws the rest of the class in, daring to stretch their chairs of light a little lower as they sense a storm building.

"There are plenty of other places to go."

"Like where?" I say.

"Where you've just come back from," Taeia adds, laughing again at reference to the sky realms.

"Somewhere you're planning to go, is it?" I add, keeping a poker face.

"When I can read the stars, you bet. I've got the feeling I won't be patronised there, leaving me to find my own kind."

"And who would they be?" Jacob queries, keeping an invisible grip on Taeia's throat until he can hardly speak.

"Outsiders like me," Taeia replies with a knowing smile. "Outsiders who don't need to fit in."

"Well, as long as you're here you'll need to fit in and *follow orders*. Your exit *isn't* in your own hands, so let's see if you're ready to venture beyond the S.P.M.A."

"Ready when you are," Taeia replies — the flawless, mixed-race skin masking dead eyes. "You create the threat and I'll smash it to pieces."

"We haven't moved to points of attack yet."

"Do you want me to show you what I've learned or not?"

"Let him, Jacob," I encourage, leaving my brother to make up his mind.

"Anything you damage you clean up," Jacob says in a sign of acceptance.

"Fair enough."

"And anyone you harm will have the right to return your friendly fire."

That draws a sigh of surprise from The Fateful Eight, suspended above us on their elongated chairs of light.

"An eye for an eye," Taeia comments with a smirk. "The sort of lesson I like."

"Then take your position. Also understand the Quij will return in blood-red fury to end your performance, if needs be."

Taeia nods, standing with his arms by his side and eyes closed ... as if he has the gift of blind sight ... a gift only given to a Winter King. "Let's go," he utters as Jacob releases the invisible grip on a lost boy's throat, and the performance begins.

18

MARKED FOR DARKNESS

With Conrad and I standing on either side of Jacob, the test of Taeia's shaky moral compass starts with a simple ritual termed 'call and response'. It's a phrase used to improve the art of reflexes to trainee witches and wizards, and as Taeia's aren't the best we go gently to start with.

He smiles as he counters our simple charms ... faint flashes of fire courtesy of the Smekelin charm, followed by us stepping things up with rings of fire, surging into life when the opposition gets close.

The Infernisi charm is a simple defensive mechanism — fire circles spinning around you that flood the enemy. The younger students adjust their chairs of light as if they're riding escalators, moving up and down to avoid getting singed by friendly fire ... fire that might get less friendly if Taeia does his usual psycho act.

Jacob spins within his rings of protective light, using his silver cane to fire out sparks that disorient Taeia — Spintz charms used as darting light with no intent to harm. So far, Taeia's keeping things together, abandoning his flashes of fire for a tornado of water he rises within: the first impressive move he makes.

To combine two charms isn't easy — water and flight charms signifying he is improving and becoming more in tune with his magical abilities. The tornado of water forces The Fateful Eight to retreat to the ceiling, getting sprayed by flecks of water for their trouble.

They don't seem to mind, excited to see older witches and wizards test their magical powers on one another. There's no real power on display, just regular moves on a stage of a troubled heir's making. We could do this all day if we needed to, but it's going to get boring soon, not to mention we're holding up a lesson we're not actually involved in.

"Let's give him something to think about," Conrad says, using the flight charm to propel him into the air, tracking Taeia's path of flight as a purple glow surrounds his tornado of water.

With Conrad floating upwards and Jacob looking on, waiting to see proof of Taeia's growth, I decide to use a favoured method of transport to trap Taeia in a small pocket of space ... near enough for the younger students to learn and me to make my point ... that arrogance usually backfires in all walks of life: magical and otherwise.

Uttering 'Whereabouts', I watch as a ball of topaz-blue light appears from my penchant ring, stretching into an archway that I vanish through moments later. The plan is simple, to appear through the window I was sitting near a while ago, precisely where Conrad's cornered Taeia. The element of surprise will force Taeia's hand, triggering any hidden venom.

His mistake on The Hallowed Lawn, firing out a mixed charm containing mild traces of dark magic, was either a sign of his unstable nature of something worse, something my re-appearance is designed to find out. My money's on another violent display — a vision of an unstable wizard losing control again.

As I walk through the tunnel of darkness, transporting me upwards to my destination outside the classroom, I get ready to appear through the window hidden within a protective curtain of light: the Verum Veras charm an ideal disguise to burst out from.

With Jacob returning his focus to The Fateful Eight, spinning them on their chairs of light to add a carnival atmosphere to proceedings, Conrad whispers 'Recindia' to neutralise Taeia's basic counterfire: a Promesiun charm surging across the classroom towards Conrad who extinguishes it with ease.

Conrad sends a web of light swarming towards Taeia, moving him closer to the window I'm about to appear through ... ready to transform my Vaspyl into chain mail, using it to wrap around the web of light to restrict our troubled heir's movements. It works perfectly, Taeia choosing the wrong response, thinking flooding the classroom will cause panic: it doesn't.

Standing in rising water isn't a new experience for me, having waded through Francis Follygrin's water chamber in my early days — the only way you could get access to a legendary recluse — and it's also a signal of the anxiety I've seen before in Taeia: an inability to adapt in real time.

Luckily for him, the opposition are the comrades he despises so much, made obvious by the cloud of fury crossing his face at the sight of me re-appearing ... a Fire Witch with an unwanted surprise morphing into life ... a blanket of chain mail wrapping around Taeia.

"Three against one!" he shouts in Jacob's direction, but

my brother's more concerned with entertaining The Fateful Eight who continue to spin on the ceiling, some of them turning a worrying shade of pale.

"You wanted to show us what you've learned," Jacob replies, frustration marking his face to signal his fading patience. "I'm still waiting."

"How can I when I've got *these two* on my case, *embarrassing me again*!"

"You can't spot a simple trap?" I say, hovering in the air near Taeia to reinforce the obvious — he just isn't that good at magical battle. He overthinks everything, losing the critical seconds needed to adapt, meaning there's never any element of surprise.

"Release him," Jacob instructs, turning his attention from his young students to Conrad and me.

He's the teacher, after all, silver cane at his side like a master studying his apprentice. Jacob's got more ability in his little finger than Taeia possesses all together, so I'm not worried about leaving him to deal with our lost boy on his own, but there's *something* about our frustrated comrade's energy.

"Release him," Jacob says again, gesturing for Conrad and me to return to the classroom floor while The Fateful Eight's ride comes to an end.

With Conrad and I doing as instructed, Jacob blows on his hands, turning at the sight of a flurry of Quij fluttering through the holes in the concrete walls. Whether it's a warning sign or not is unclear, particularly as the tiny, luminous insects have returned to their soft, colourful glows. Either way, the Quij are a weapon if needed although I doubt they will be.

"Keep an eye on the other students," Jacob adds as we return to the classroom floor alongside him, watching as

Taeia chooses to stay suspended in mid-air. "I've got a feeling what he's about to show us isn't going to fill us with joy."

He doesn't need to say anymore because I'm thinking the same thing; it's something about the *way* Taeia hovers, suddenly more confident as if he knows something we don't. *Does* he know his destiny? Has he *always* sensed it? The reason why he's fought so hard to not belong here?

More importantly, has Casper always known? If so, we've been kept in the dark again although I find that hard to believe. I mean, after everything we went through two years ago, the one thing the adults *definitely* learnt was the limitations of secrecy.

It's more likely that secrecy's remained about the sky realms — an invisible tie connecting a recently deceased king and the boy who raises his arms now ... messiah like ... *just like* Thylas did during his final act ... drawing the hundred platforms of light into the sky to circle him. It was a death ritual filled with 'blind visions' — visions that showed us a wizard filled with fury astride a black Williynx, storming towards the white fortress of Devreack.

"That doesn't look good," Conrad whispers, uttering 'Velinis' as a bubble of tanzanite light surrounds us, including the eight young classmates who start to look a *lot* less comfortable.

"What's he doing?" Katie Follygrin asks, the most competitive of the students, about to learn the dangers of a desire for domination.

"Stretching," Olin Zucklewick replies with an unimpressed smile: the short, clever boy the others are paying more attention to. Olin's got something about him, all right, including an intuition he shares with my brother — probably the reason both of them look calm as strings of light stretch from Taeia's outstretched arms ... strands of light that filter through the small holes in the concrete walls, darting up as they do.

The sight of the Quij turning a darker colour signals we're in for another show, but not of the good kind. With Jacob watching silently, lifting his hand as I try to suggest the need for protection, the next phase begins ... a strange sound coming from Taeia as he closes his eyes.

"Bloody hell," Conrad whispers. "He's *doing* it."

"Doing what?" I ask.

"The incantations Thylas was doing before he died. *The language. The secret spells.*"

How Conrad's worked this out is beyond me, but when Jacob closes *his* eyes I know we've got trouble. Part of me wants to speak but silence dominates now, the strange words spoken by Taeia sending The Fateful Eight into a trance, heads lowered as they struggle to keep their eyes open.

"The silent influence," I whisper to Conrad, nudging Leah Creswell who lifts her head momentarily before it drops again. "He's got power all right."

"He's *connecting*," Conrad says, looking on edge all of a sudden. "He's connecting to the sky realms."

"Through the strands of light?" I ask, tracing the light through the holes in the wall, and seeing a sight confirming Conrad's theory. The strands of light streaming from Taeia's hands cover The Cendryll's skylight until the sunlight's replaced with *something else*: a familiar triangle of allegiance throbbing with life and stopping witches and wizards in their tracks.

The sound of doors banging open throughout The Cendryll makes Taeia open his eyes, sending a venomous stare my way as he says, "Who's the lost boy now?"

With only Jacob standing outside our protective bubble of light, watching Taeia's every move as the blood-red Quij circle around his silver cane, the expected explosion of fury follows, but not directed at any individual. Instead, the heir who's finally found his calling shouts 'DISINERIS', glaring at the concrete wall that explodes around us, fragments bouncing off our protective bubble of light.

"Jacob! Move!" I shout to my brother who seems to be in his own trance, until he whips his cane into the air, whispering 'Fora' to create his own force field of protection. The cane stays in the air like a rifle zoned in on its target, but no counterfire comes, Jacob's intense expression struggling with something he doesn't articulate: a reality we've all tried to ignore.

Taeia *is* the new Winter King, meaning he has the right to leave the S.P.M.A. without consequence now. He doesn't have to wait to be assessed by the teacher he clearly despises, laughing as the light flowing from his hands fills his body until he's a beacon of change: a boy on a mission to an awaiting kingdom.

"What do we do?" Conrad asks from inside our Velinis charm.

"What *can* we do?" I reply, glancing at the catatonic state the young students are in — *definitely* not a good omen. "We can't stop him leaving now he's proven what Thylas always knew. He belongs *up there*."

"So, we just let him leave?"

"Yes," comes Jacob's reply: a brother who doesn't take his eyes off a king in waiting. "We let him leave."

"And if he tries an unfriendly farewell."

"We accelerate his exit," Jacob says, turning to me for a second, the look on his face one I've seen few times in my life. He looks burdened again — the way he was when mum lost her way and, later, when he realised the Society was on the verge of war.

"Okay," I say, wanting to reassure him in some way. We've always been close and I'm getting better at knowing when to retreat, trusting his famous intuition.

"What if the Society elders don't let him leave?" Conrad asks, manoeuvring the sleeping students behind him as Taeia floats past, flooded with the white light of the realm calling him.

As he moves past us, offering a final glance of contempt, I reply, "It's time to find out."

With Taeia passing through the wall, guided by the strands of light connected to his hands, I utter 'Undilum', releasing us from the Velinis charm before I create another one for our sleeping students.

With Conrad and I free to watch the passing of a problem in the making, Jacob snaps out of his troubled state, joining us near the shattered wall. From our fifth-floor vantage point, we've got a perfect view of the skylight flooded with the same white light filling Taeia's body, as well as the crowd of Society members gathered on the floors below. The sight of a unified Society army fills me with hope, arms lifted towards the floating body of a comrade few wanted in their midst.

Casper's the person holding my attention ... the man who decided to let his nephew in ... hoping it would help to alleviate the tornado raging in him. From the look on Casper's face, he isn't convinced but at least he tried and, who knows, maybe Jacob saving Taeia's life will stay with him — plus the fact Casper saved him from a life of exile in the above-ground world.

"He's got a battle ahead of him yet," Jacob states,

pointing his silver cane towards The Cendryll's skylight. "He might be destined for Devreack but his path won't be clear."

"Kelph?" I say, remembering our meeting with the leaders of the pirate economy, and the Bloodseekers who lined the sky on our return.

"Kelph or any of the other groups waiting in the wings."

"What did he see in the stars, Jacob?" Conrad asks as The Cendryll rests in silence, each floor lined with a unified circle of witches and wizards, preparing to defend what they hold dear. "When you sat with him on the skylight at night?"

"He never said," Jacob replies, taking off the Society tie binding him to the eight sleeping students, heads lowered in their protective bubble of light. "But he spent hours firing out strings of light into the night sky, getting calmer each time he did. I joined him when I sensed he was onto something ... the *smile* that crossed his face on the final night up there ... like something in the air had entered into his body."

"And the last night you were up there was the night Thylas died," I add.

"The passing of the torch to an unworthy wizard," Jacob comments, "meaning we've got another battle on our hands."

19

DESPERATE MEASURES

With arms raised in silence, the Society army standing in unified circles wait for Taeia's move. The Cendryll's rarely been so quiet, sombre moments only occurring during death rituals. I'm hoping we won't have anyone to bury today, peering through the shattered wall with Conrad and Jacob as Taeia floats higher, looking like a demigod connected to the heavens. I doubt heaven's where he's headed, the bitter expression and dead eyes a sign of what we've got in store.

I wonder now if this is why Taeia couldn't ignite the magic within him — all those days of training seemingly having no impact on him beyond basic spells. He never belonged here, as he kept telling us. He wanted to be expelled because he knew the S.P.M.A. wasn't home, suggesting he always sensed an *elsewhere* calling him.

The silence holds as Taeia reaches the base of The Cendryll's skylight ... the Quij called away by the small circle Casper and Farraday are standing in. It's a standoff where neither party wants to make the first move. The S.P.M.A. is all about peace, after all, unless battle is absolutely necessary, and it doesn't look like Taeia's looking for a battle.

He's looking for something though, arms stretched out like a fallen messiah as he hangs suspended near the skylight, flooded with visions in the skies, a shimmering image of interconnected realms above his head. It's the first time he looks truly *powerful* ... the light charging from his hands, connecting the walls of a magical faculty for all eventualities.

"He's not going to leave without a statement," Conrad states, checking on the catatonic figures of the Fateful Eight who stand motionless, none the wiser to the unfolding events.

"A cowardly attack probably," I say, adjusting my position as a fragment of the stone wall digs into my leg.

"On who?"

"Someone he's got a problem with."

"Casper, then," Conrad adds. "He's the one who brought him in, deciding to train him properly."

"Hardly a reason to carry a grudge."

"It's the humiliation Taeia remembers," Jacob says, throwing his cane into the air to transform it into a mirror: the magical benefits of morphing steel. "It's like he looks into a mirror and sees all of his failures, and the people responsible for them."

"That sounds healthy," I quip, wondering why Jacob's staring in the mirror — as if he sees something in there — another secret power my brother's decided not to mention. I'm also wondering where Kaira is, assuming she's still in her above-ground home at 12 Spyndall Street: a sign she's still in two minds about returning to Society duty.

"It's the root of all his anger," Jacob adds. "The belief the world has turned on him, and now he's got the power to do something about it."

"The world turning on him?" Conrad queries, shaking some debris out of his copper-blonde hair. "You saved his life and Casper gave him a second chance."

"Disturbed people don't see things that way. Taeia's a narcissist, only able to see himself in the mirror: his responses to events and his feelings. Everyone else is a shadow but some shadows haunt him — the shadows who caused the wounds."

"Do you actually *see* anything in the mirror?" I ask, getting a sense my brother's keeping another gift from me.

"A boy with a hollow heart," Jacob adds cryptically, "desperately trying to fill it."

"Maybe he should focus on trying to heal it," Conrad adds as a hum lifts around us: the sign a Winter King is about to make a dramatic exit.

"A focus on healing requires humility, Conrad, something Taeia clearly lacks."

"How long before we've got a problem in the skies?"

"The moment he makes his mark, wherever that may be. He certainly likes the attention, doesn't he?" Jacob adds, looking on as Taeia crosses his arms, causing the light flooding through him to spread out until he appears in illuminated form ... mirror images of him hovering in mid-air ... the narcissistic streak Jacob mentioned coming to the fore.

"Is he going to do anything or just hover there all day?" I say, wishing we could just send him blasting through the skylight — our own version of farewell.

"He's waiting for a reaction he's not going to get, so he'll do something to rub salt into the wound," Jacob comments, "making Casper feel like he's failed."

"Wanting the last word."

"Yep, although when has Casper Renn ever lost a battle?"

"Here we go," Conrad adds as the mirror images of Taeia float closer, sparks of light firing off each one as The Cendryll holds strong ... arms raised in the air as their perfect circles wait for the command ... to study or strike.

"I say we join them," I suggest, feeling a little guilty for spectating on potential carnage. "Nothing mad but to show our support."

"Let's wait for Taeia to make his move," Jacob suggests, offering the familiar brotherly wisdom. "Appearing now might trigger a reaction we don't want."

"Fair enough," I agree, watching as a king in the waiting remains illuminated by the flood of light surrounding him, eyes closed and arms crossed as if he's leading a spiritual awakening. He looks ridiculous in some ways, but he's undoubtedly dangerous so I wait to blast into action the moment he makes his move: a move that surprises us all.

As the holograph images of Taeia reach Casper's circle of resistance, each Society soldier is lifted off the ground, including Kaira's dad and Farraday. It's a sight that makes me gasp, stunned to see three of the most powerful wizards in our midst losing control ... or at least that's what it looks like ... Casper's circle of resistance immobile as they rise ... the sight of the Quij fluttering *away* from them a sign that's something's *very* wrong.

"He *can't* be controlling them," Conrad whispers, his face reddening in anger as he eases through the hole in the shattered wall.

Jacob attempts to stop Conrad, but the boy I've fallen for is a sky rider who doesn't wait in the wings. Maybe it's the sight of Taeia filling with power and potentially turning it on us. Alternatively, he's *draining* The Cendryll of its magical energy. Either way, it's a bad sign and sitting here watching isn't going to help.

"Guppy," Jacob says as I follow Conrad through the shattered wall, almost within reach of a wizard with a *massive* chip on his shoulder.

"We jump into his shield of light and get a reaction," Conrad says, keeping his eyes fixed on Taeia's cross-armed figure, eyes closed and reminding me more and more of Thylas' last moments in the sky. Whatever magic he's connected to exists between our world and the sky realms, because it's powerful enough to suspend a small Society army in mid-air — powerful enough to draw a flood of Williynx bursting through the doors lining the ground floor.

I'm reassured by the sight of our feathered friends resting on the shoulders of our comrades, feeling even better when each Williynx spreads its wings, creating a protective shield above the heads of Casper's small army: a competing force field to counter whatever charms Taeia's using.

Jacob joins us as the shield of feathers stretches upwards, reaching the boy with a messiah complex who opens his eyes suddenly.

"They're *black*," Conrad whispers, looking for any sight of his turquoise Williynx amongst our feathered friends. "His eyes are black."

"We can write off the idea of him heading to Devreack then," Jacob adds, placing one foot over the edge as the shield of Williynx feathers spreads further, until little can be seen between a suspended enemy and an expanding Society force.

Without another word, Jacob steps off our shattered landing, falling into the shield of Williynx feathers until he's out of sight, joining our comrades protected from Taeia's growing powers. Conrad and I share a look before we also step off, falling into a multi-coloured blanket of feathers blessed with their own powerful magic.

Whatever the Williynx have in mind, I'm confident it will be powerful enough to protect us from the force dragging The Cendryll collective upwards ... now hovering with a greater level of control ... no longer puppets in a wicked dance. We find Jacob hovering alongside Casper and Farraday: an old alliance re-forming against a different threat.

"What's happening?" I ask as Conrad and I take our places alongside Jacob.

"Competing forces," Farraday says, shaking away his thinning, brown hair to reveal scars from the last war. "Taeia's connected with the sky realms now, flooded with the power this brings. He hasn't learnt enough to know he's competing with a *whole* universe, much vaster than the one he's about to reign over."

"So, he poses no threat?" Conrad asks.

"Enough of a threat to track his exit out of here," Casper adds, "which is what we'll do when he realises he's on the verge of another humiliation."

"It looks like he's winning the battle at the moment."

"An illusion only an inexperienced wizard would fall for," Casper states as he nods to the collected Cendryll army, and the counter move begins.

WITH THE SHIELD OF MULTI-COLOURED WILLIYNX FEATHERS rising higher, closing in on Taeia's suspended figure, our own light show begins ... single feathers at first that dissolve in a flood of light surrounding our nemesis until they reappear as rings of light, moving towards Taeia's throat. It's a simple trick that Taeia falls for, drunk with power and the mistaken idea he's got the upper hand.

As the rings of light tighten around his throat, he gives into his violent side, sending a blizzard of counter fire towards the skylight, shattering the vision of the sky realms he's heading towards: a coward looking for the exit.

"He's not going to be much of a king if a few feathers take him down," I whisper to Conrad, but I know this is only the beginning.

"What now?" Jacob asks, reaching out to touch the fire-red Williynx resting on his shoulder, our majestic comrades maintaining smaller forms for now.

"We track his path to the sky realms," Casper says as he gives another nod to his army.

"Simple reconnaissance," Farraday adds, giving me a knowing glance. "No false moves: harder days are ahead of us."

It's a comment that sums up where we are: a magical world prepared to protect our allies who are fighting various enemies in the skies. I've been here before, joining the battle slowly when the S.P.M.A. was under threat. It's different now and *feels* different in some ways, the sense of stepping beyond what you know to protect what you don't yet understand.

"He's got no idea what's waiting for him," Casper adds as Taeia turns the force field of light towards the shattered skylight, blasting upwards into the skies as he races to the stars, tracked by an army conditioned for war.

20

RACE TO THE STARS

The race to the stars is another experience I'm unlikely to forget — a spectacular vision of a Society army blazing through the sky on lines of fire as Taeia blasts ahead, increasingly cornered by sky soldiers coming from all directions ... not into battle but ensuring no conflict happens as the heir to the sky realms seeks his channel to freedom. The Williynx maintain their small forms, probably aware that expanding into battle flight could trigger an unwanted reaction.

Conflict isn't the aim, judging by the way the Society elders cruise on their carpets of fire, monitoring Taeia's every move as he storms upwards, arms still placed across his chest with his eyes closed. It's the first time he's looked regal, calm and totally unconcerned with the Society force tracking him ... a bitter wizard ordained by the skies he's rushing towards.

It isn't until the sky channels open that I realise what Casper meant — about Taeia having no idea what's waiting for him. Kaira described it as shooting stars and twisted light, and that's what happens now ... a shower of stars exploding in every direction, framed by twisting, multi-coloured light as various sky channels open, competing for Taeia's powers.

With Taeia wrapped in his own cocoon of light, I race through the sky alongside Conrad and Jacob, using my feet to direct my travel along the pathway of fire. There are no ropes of fire to whip up a fury, our hands free to release defensive charms if necessary, but I doubt they will be — this isn't about the defence of the S.P.M.A. but the fate of a boy born to reign.

As the explosion of stars increase in their intensity, Taeia opens his eyes, darkened by the release of a hidden power. He studies each channel of twisted light headed his way. The arc of white light stretching towards him has to be from Devreack ... The Winter King's fortress ready to anoint its new heir ... but Taeia shifts away, darting through the air on no visible path, towards the mouth of red light looking to swallow him.

"Kelph," Jacob says as he pivots his body to mirror Taeia's movements. "Got to be."

"I knew he'd back away from Devreack," Conrad adds, swerving left on his path of fire as a shower of golden stars threaten to wrap him in their magical glow. "He's got Kelph written all over him; a pirate Prince with revenge on his mind."

"No false moves," Farraday repeats, appearing alongside me on a circle of spinning light. "We see him out beyond our boundaries, that's all. Remember, we have no claim over the sky realms and interfering will bring problems we don't need."

"But leaving him to abandon his fate guarantees problems," I counter, hovering near Farraday as Taeia closes in on the mouth of red light.

"Problems not of our making and only addressed if necessary," Farraday adds.

"Sounds like you won't be fighting when it kicks off up there, then," Conrad comments, adjusting his feet to hover alongside us.

"Thylas called on you for a reason, seeing something in the young that we've already witnessed: an ability to navigate mysteries beyond the realm of adults. It's the reason other young Night Rangers will join you when the time comes."

"Help will arrive when needed," Casper adds, appearing out of nowhere as his nephew closes on his choice, darting away from the other twisted channels of light, desperate to claim him as their own. "It's the Society way, but for now we can only look on from a safe distance, watching what we all expected to see: a troubled wizard choosing a troubled path."

"At least you tried, Casper," I offer to Kaira's dad as our small group stands united.

One of the lines of Society surveillance frame Taeia's exit, holding their positions as the vision no one wanted to see is played out ... a flurry of black Williynx appearing out of the mouth of red light, accompanied by a wild clan dressed from the waist down ... shoulder length hair lifting as their black Williynx spin towards their new leader: the pirate army of Kelph.

The sight of black Williynx makes me feel sad in a way, the memory of my first trip to Gilweean washing over me now. A carousel of colour touched the sky that day, flying over the rainbow waterfall as they shape shifted into massive forms. Williynx feathers are linked to the colours of The Devenant: beautiful colours that act as a reminder of how blessed we are to exist in a world of wonder.

Black Williynx don't fit this picture *at all*, reinforcing that fact we're *elsewhere* now, reaching the boundaries of our magical world as we look onto another: a fragile triangle of allegiance about to be thrown into chaos. With Devreack forming the axis of the sky realms, we're going to be travelling towards the stars soon, because the white fortress protected by one hundred paths lies empty now — protected by the huge, white Williynx that welcomed us.

Yes, each of the hundred paths acts as a defence mechanism, but without a king on the throne it's more vulnerable, made worse given the fact an anointed king has chosen to align himself with the enemy: pirates keen to turn the tide of power in their favour.

"I knew it would end this way," Casper replies after a lengthy silence. "Some of us are marked for darkness, no matter what magic is used to avert this. It means you'll be put in dangerous situations again, Guppy: you, Conrad, Jacob and the others."

"Kaira?" I ask, deciding it's time to find out what my best friend's going to do.

"Still deciding," Casper replies, looking on as Taeia comes alive as he mounts a black Williynx, punching the air in triumph as he enters the mouth of red light, engulfing him in a world that might not worship him. "We asked too much of you last time and now Taeia's made his choice, we'll require your assistance again. Thylas has chosen you for a reason, something he saw in his final visions. As soon as Taeia makes his mark, you'll get the signal to help."

"From who?" Jacob asks as we hover in the sky.

"From whoever needs us," Casper adds, ever the elegant, grand wizard. "Devreack is the axis of the sky realms, but the surrounding realms are equally important: Whistluss and Zordeya particularly so — realms controlled by warrior women who have defended their territory for centuries."

I smile at the idea of a king's fortress reliant on female power. "So now we just wait and see?"

"That's right, Guppy," Farraday adds as he picks up his pace, deciding it's time for him to have his own fun in the skies. "Carry on with life until the call comes. Anyway, my scars are burning so time for a little remedy in Rebel's Rest. Anyone care to join me?"

I'm off before Jacob and Conrad can respond, wanting to shake off the feeling of being in Taeia's presence, and the thought of what's to come.

"Come on then!" I shout to the others, urging the Society elders to loosen up a little as Jacob and Conrad swerve towards me with reactivated ropes of light. "Unless you're too old, that is."

Casper's smile triggers the race, the Society legend darting out of sight before re-appearing ahead of me. He streaks ahead with the Society adults in hot pursuit, rare laughter from a magical collective wanting to hold on to peace and wonder for a moment longer — each of us conscious that it may have to take second place in the days to come.

With Jacob, Conrad and I falling further behind, I think of Kaira holed up in 12 Spyndall Street and Lucy and Noah who'll be filled in soon. I hope they join us in the sky realms when we're called: an expanded army of young witches and wizards helping to keep a fragile universe intact.

We'll be on a mercy mission of sorts, hoping to guide Taeia towards the mercy hidden within him, or at least that's *my* hope. Few witches and wizards are *completely* evil, and although Taeia's eyes turned black when a new power flooded through him, I remember the lost, bitter boy on The Hallowed Lawn, crippled by a feeling of inadequacy.

There's a chance to save the kingdom of Devreack yet, so I dart through the skies with my brother and favourite boy wizard by my side, smiling at the sight of the adults lighting up the skies with the S.P.M.A. logo: a symbol of everything that's precious in my life. The sky realms are precious in their own way, the memory of Thylas spinning his final vision to highlight what's in store.

It might not be *our* magical universe but it's connected nonetheless — a reminder of how quickly things can fracture and what's needed when they do. Also, Thylas was a Renn: the family who've done so much for me. If anything, I owe it to Kaira, Casper and Philomeena to go to battle again — a thanks to the family who saved me from a life of neglect.

At the sight of the Williynx expanding in the skies, expanding their wings in a sign they're ready for a race of their own, I whistle to Laieya who swoops near, climbing on as she does so. There's no sign of Conrad's Williynx so I fly towards him, whistling for him to climb on which he does with ease.

Jacob's next and the three of us surge towards the outline of Zilom ... a suspended stage of light looking like a lighthouse from up here. Zilom is the touchdown point that wins the race and as we near, I whisper for Laieya to release a flurry of powder-blue feathers: a sign we're closing in on the Society elders who streak through the sky.

"Cheating!" Farraday shouts at the sight of us flying past on our feathered friend.

"Quick thinking!" I reply with a salute before we free fall together, spinning like ballerinas towards the sky tower of

Zilom, edging ahead of Casper and Farraday who touch down seconds later.

"Get some remedy down you, old friend," Casper says to Farraday with a smile, the dark-blue suit a mark of his elegance. "The itching season is upon us."

I know what that means, all right, my scars always burning worse as winter approaches.

"I think cheating means you lot pay for the drinks," Farraday growls as he rubs at the scars on his face. "Couldn't beat a group of old wizards so you whistle for a Williynx's help."

"Well, we could have beaten you without Laieya but didn't want to embarrass you," Conrad jokes, ducking as Farraday swipes at him. "I mean, *kids* beating legends in a race."

"Kids about to get a hiding," Farraday jokes, pretending to look angry as he puts Jacob in a headlock.

"It wasn't *my* idea," Jacob says, looking happy he's escaped a morning's teaching for one day, which makes me wonder how The Fateful Eight are doing — probably mute in their bubble of protection unless someone's bumped into them that is.

Either way, there'll be no lessons for the rest of the day because Rebel's Rest calls at Farraday's request: a teacher in his own right who's struggling with old scars. He's had his own class to deal with recently, Taeia's ex Night Ranger crew who've had the pleasure of his company.

Apparently, Farraday's been throwing creatures at them to shock them into submission, draining their arrogance and pushing them to the edge of their magical powers.

"Tell you what," I say to our old friend and comrade. "We'll get the drinks in if you tell us what's happening with Alice, Mae and Fillian."

"Deal," Farraday says, brushing the thinning, brown hair away from his face, "although be prepared for a ghost story."

"You haven't killed them, have you?" Conrad jokes as the remaining group of Society soldiers touch down, lining the sky tower surrounded by suspended rain.

"No remedy, no story" Farraday adds with a mischievous smile, uttering 'Disira' before he vanishes out of sight, soon to appear in The Singing Quarter where he'll find magical concoctions for old wounds.

"I'll take care of your sleeping students," Casper says to Jacob, offering his hand as he does so. "Thanks for your efforts with Taeia. It wasn't my most popular decision but I had to try."

"He's family at the end of the day," Jacob replies, conscious of everything Casper's done for us and our mum. "It's hard to give up on family."

"Indeed, Jacob, but it looks like Taeia's given up on himself, and in the realm of Kelph that could be fatal. Anyway, Farraday's looking forward to your company in Rebel's Rest so I'll say goodbye for now."

"How long before the skies rumble?" I ask, looking up at the S.P.M.A. logo sparkling in the sky: a sign help is nearby.

"Days," Casper adds as the other Society elders tumble off the edge of the sky tower, making their own dramatic return to more familiar territory. "Weeks at best. When the stars fall out of the sky, we'll know it's time. Above all, Devreack must be protected; that's our only mission."

"You're coming?" Conrad prompts.

"I'll be close by," Casper adds with a look I've seen before ... of a man gifted in the art of battle, brushing his hand against a strand of suspended rain to return to his own kingdom — The Cendryll — and eight young students who've had their first brush with danger.

21

A QUESTION OF DESTINY

Rebel's Rest is as lively as always, both inside and out on the streets of The Singing Quarter. It's the place you head to when you want to park Society business, ready to indulge in a bit of fun. It's also where Lucy and Noah reappear, needing some alone time after our return from the sky realms. They're a new couple, trying to balance romance and rapidly escalating events.

Jalem, Ilina and Harvey wave us over — our trio of friends who've chosen safer adventures in separate magical faculties. They love hearing all about our Night Ranger adventures, particularly Harvey who's a ball of excitement when we get to them.

It's been less about Night Ranging than wizard taming lately, leading to a well-needed break at Farraday's request. There's also the fact that Farraday's struggling with his scars, the burning sensation he mentioned more obvious when we find a table. Harvey's over straight away, jigging his way through a crowd of wizards, pointing at something I can't make out.

"Nutters, the lot of them," Harvey says as he sits down

alongside us, annoyed when one of the panelled walls spins outwards, sending a bumbling witch falling into his lap.

"Fumbunction!" the heavily made up witch shouts, aimed at no one in particular.

"I attract the best ones," Harvey adds as he gathers himself, rotating his neck as if he's been injured by the experience.

"You've always had a thing for the older ladies," Ilina comments as she glides over, ever the elegant specimen in all frocks and flowing hair.

Harvey's got a thing for her but she's *way* out of his league, only a year older but clearly not interested in him. Harvey's sweet but *manic,* unable to sit still for more than a few seconds, tapping his feet as he grabs a floating tray, then whistling to get Zoe Tallis' attention: Noah's old obsession.

Seeing we've just walked in, Zoe ignores Harvey's request, sending a tray flying his way out of annoyance. Whistling at a girl rarely goes down well.

"I've got a thing for *sophisticated women,*" Harvey replies to Ilina's teasing, giving her a wink before he stands. He claps for service this time before another tray connects with his head, sending him tumbling to the floor.

Bellows of laughter fill the room, followed by a spontaneous song for Harvey's benefit. He doesn't look impressed, nursing his bruised head as the song blasts through the room.

"You need to work on your moves, son," Farraday says as he utters 'Flori', smiling at the sight of a rose appearing in the palm of his hand. He blows on his hand to send the rose floating towards an older barmaid, singing along as she sends jars of remedies flying across the bar.

When the rose reaches her, darting away from grasping

hands, she puts it in her hair and sends Farraday a wink: a sign our order is in.

"Whenever I wink I get ignored or slapped," Harvey says in a sulk.

"It's all part of the art," Farraday replies, rubbing the scars on his neck and face. "You've got to choose your moment carefully, executing with sincerity."

"I'm *always* sincere."

"Clapping and whistling," Ilina says as Jalem arrives, the third member of our trio of friends normally covered in powder from various experiments. "It's disrespectful and childish."

Harvey's obviously not in the mood for a lesson so I change the subject, asking Farraday about the 'ghost story' he mentioned — his way of explaining what's happening with Taeia's ex crew: Alice, Mae and Fillian.

"A little dance with the dead," Farraday replies.

"Eh?" Harvey pipes up, almost falling off his chair again when Farraday swipes at him.

As our tray of remedies arrives, Farraday slides Harvey's towards him. "Drink up and shut up, son; I'm burning all over and need a dozen of these to feel normal again."

Sensing he probably *will* get slapped if he replies, Harvey does as he's told, leaving Farraday to add a little detail to the 'ghost story'.

"The Orium Circle has left it up to us to decide their fate."

"The Cendryll members, you mean?" Jacob asks, sipping his Jysyn Juice.

"Yep, and Casper's come up with a solution."

"Not another battle with a Williynx?" I comment, remembering how close Taeia came to death on The Hallowed Lawn.

"No, more like a meeting with ghosts."

"Ghosts...?" Conrad says, looking a little puzzled.

"Yes, Conrad. Dead legends to give them the creeps."

"Why?"

"A reminder of how lucky they are to still be with us."

"And then...?" Noah prompts, burping after he gulps down his colourful remedy.

"Then they'll be covered in the ashes of the dead."

"To decide their future?" Lucy prompts.

"Yep."

"A bit grim if you ask me," I say.

"Not as grim as what's waiting for us in the sky realms."

"Thanks."

"My pleasure. Anyway, enough about the fallen trio; let's talk about what you *really* want to know."

"Okay. What's Taeia's plan now he's joined forces with Kelph?" Conrad asks.

"To slowly dominate the surrounding realms, which he'll have a problem with because most of them are loyal to Devreack — empty throne or not. Disturbing The Winter King's fortress disrupts everything, although Taeia's too blind to see this."

"Will he ever see it?" Conrad asks, reaching for Harvey's orange remedy.

Harvey shrugs, still sulking after his embarrassing episode with Zoe Tallis: a girl with a habit of humiliating boys, it seems.

"Who knows," Farraday replies as he grabs the floating trays of remedies, downing the lot without taking a breath. Less irritated by his scars, he relaxes a little — even looking a little guilty for his harsh treatment of Harvey. "Don't worry, son, you'll get the knack of girls one day," he offers, snapping his fingers to create a heart of light. "It's all about matters of the heart. If you can unlock what's hidden inside, you'll turn into a Casanova."

"That'll be the day," Jalem teases, giving Harvey a comical hug to cheer him up.

The hug turns into a playful wrestling match until Ilina creates a Cympgus — a rectangle of light on the floor that gets rid of them. "I'm not in the mood," is the only explanation we get from our elegant friend, before she adds, "What if Taeia doesn't see that attacking Devreack is likely to backfire on him?"

"Then he pays the price," Farraday comments, clicking his fingers to turn the heart of light into a coffin. "Destroying the throne of Devreack is like smashing The Devenant, almost impossible when a colossal army rises up to defend it: an invisible army he won't see coming."

"But Thylas' vision," I say, watching as the coffin of light morphs into the very vision we saw. "A vision of a boy-king charging towards his destiny, you mean," Farraday comments, his scars looking less raw now. "An incomplete vision because Thylas couldn't see what happened next ... his gift of 'blind sight' fading as he moved towards death."

"So it's wrong?" Noah queries, jumping when Harvey and Jalem appear alongside us, both covered in snow, suggesting their wrestling match has taken them to The Winter Quarter and back again.

"It's limited," Farraday replies, gesturing for us to look out of the window. "What do you see when you look out onto the streets?"

"Witches and wizards moving about," Lucy replies, "some vanishing through portals of light."

"And what *can't* you see?" Farraday prompts, getting a puzzled look from us all — except Jacob.

"Where they're going," my brother says. "You can't see

where they're going and why; it's half a picture absent of projection and intention."

"Spoken like a true teacher," I tease but Jacob's right, of course: we *don't* know what happens next beyond Thylas' final vision, particularly Taeia's intention. Is he on a mission of destruction? If so, where's his army? It's just him, floating in Farraday's mock-up of what we saw in the Devreack sky, roaring with his arm raised, charging towards the throne he's turned his back on.

Also, why return to destroy a place you never wanted in the first place? To prove you can ... that you're more powerful than anything else? He might be infused with new powers, but he's hardly a warrior — or is he now he's found a way of drawing immense power from the skies? It's all too much to think about right now so I sip on my Jysyn Juice, enjoying the sweet taste of a remedy for bravery.

Bravery isn't what we're lacking, foresight is, or at least the foresight to see what's raging through Taeia now. A puzzle that makes me hungry all of a sudden. We haven't eaten for hours so I decided on making this visit a short one, needing my bed and the treats I can find in Founders' Quad.

"One thing I do know," Farraday comments, unbuttoning the brown waistcoat that's holding his belly in. "It's going to take the power of the young, the experience of the old and the ashes of the dead to reign Taeia in."

"And will that be enough?" I ask, sensing the answer.

"Time will tell, Guppy," Farraday says, glancing at the glittering vision hovering above our table — of a meeting awaiting us in the secret universe in the skies.

22

HALLOWED GROUND

The meeting with ghosts takes place on The Hallowed Lawn a few hours later. The ashes of the dead rest on the immaculate grass, rising before they spin into visions of the sacrifices they made: Smyck saving Kaira's life; the sky urchins swarming over Erent Koll's body, and Isiah Renn whipping Kaira out of a blood chamber.

Kaira has rejoined us after taking time out above ground, giving her time to think over the idea of Society duty. I understand her concern about stepping into the fray again. Night Ranging can be tense but rarely presents any serious threat, something that can't be said for the sky realms.

At least it gives me a chance to fill Kaira in on Taeia's escape, but first we've got to see if Alice, Mae and Fillian are going to get another chance: Taeia's ex-crew members looking terrified as they huddle together.

Kaira stands alongside me, offering me a smile that suggests she's made up her mind, but that could be just my imagination. She hasn't given any signs either way, but she will in time, stepping into battle again or keeping her distance — a distance that returns when her dad explains the purpose of the ritual to a frightened trio.

"Beauty and unity are not merely words but the principles we live by," Casper says to Fillian, Mae and Alice who keep their heads lowered. "I wear my scars with pride because I fought to save the most stunning place in existence. What you did with Taeia, firing on your comrades, *disgraced* the sacrifices other underage members have given to keep us safe. Now, it's time for you to step into the ashes."

"*What?*" Fillian says with a look of pure fear.

He thinks 'stepping into the ashes' means they're going to be *reduced* to ashes, but it won't turn out that way thankfully. It means their fate's going to be decided by dead legends — legends ready to discover what 'lives under the skin' as Farraday likes to put it.

It's a gruesome version of The Web of Azryllis: a surveillance system assessing intentions. Alice, Mae and Fillian's intentions are unclear so this is the test they've got. Farraday stands motionless alongside us, looking completely unconcerned which I take to be a good sign. He was like this when Taeia faced the white Williynx he attacked, and that worked out okay.

Things have escalated since then, obviously, but that isn't down to Alice, Mae and Fillian's actions. They were just following along, lost in the power of their leader who's made his escape. We watch from the sidelines, all hoping this is just another friendly warning, but how friendly can dead legends be if they feel disrespected?

"Don't look so worried, Guppy," Farraday says. "It's about them realising the knock-on effect of what they've done."

"I thought you would have drilled that home, Farraday," I say, raising my eyebrows.

Our old comrade has ways of getting his point across, including using a Zombul to release evil creatures. Shock and awe is Farraday's preferred teaching method — more shock when he feels people are stepping out of line — which makes me wonder why this 'ash of the dead' ritual is necessary.

"The Society elders voted and this is what they've decided."

"Being smothered by ashes," Noah comments, ruffling his long, black hair as he shuffles on the sidelines.

"Always so dramatic, Noah," Farraday replies, offering us a vial of Semphul: a remedy for hunger.

I'm starving so grab the vial.

"It's more of an *adventure* than a punishment," Farraday adds with a smile, gulping down another vial of the hunger remedy.

"I doubt they see it that way," Lucy states, nudging Noah to stop his odd shuffling motion.

"What they see or think isn't important, Lucy; what they *learn* is."

"Which is?"

"*Loyalty* if it's still in them. Any magician who can be turned so easily is a problem. The ashes will test their loyalty, and the rest will take care of itself."

"And if they prove not to be loyal?" Jacob asks.

Farraday throws the empty vial in the air, using a Fora charm to keep it floating above us. It's his way of avoiding Jacob's question, suggesting disloyalty doesn't have a happy ending.

"Everything was planned from the beginning, I suppose," Conrad says, changing the subject. He doesn't seem worried about Mae, Alice and Fillian's safety, helping me relax a little. "How we were asked to help Taeia before we travelled to the sky realms, as if you already knew the outcome."

"You could put it that way, but we will always operate as one."

"So, you're relying on us more?"

"We're forced to, Conrad, because there's only so much a person can give. Eventually, the scars become too much and the burden too great: the price we pay for peace."

"You've given enough, Farraday," I say, remembering how he carried a lethal artefact in crippling pain, fighting on when the scars appeared.

"Not quite, but it won't be long. Power fades from us all in the end, even the great witches and wizards."

"A shame it won't fade from the one we've got a problem with," Conrad comments.

"Is there any good left in Taeia?" Kaira asks, remaining distant. "Or is he a lost cause?"

Sweeping his thinning, brown hair back, Farraday raises his right arm to the unsettled sky, sending a beam of light shooting upwards. As the light spreads, forming into the S.P.M.A. logo, he replies, "Buried deep within him, maybe, but power reveals us all, Kaira."

"So, you *are* expecting a battle up there?" I ask, raising my arm to send my own beam of light skyward, adding a topaz-blue outline to the S.P.M.A. logo.

"A battle to restore balance, yes. The leaders of each sky realm will decide if war is necessary; we're there to stop someone causing problems for us all."

As the others send their own light beam into the rumbling sky, I consider the idea of a rescue mission. Rescue wasn't the plan I had in mind, but I'm not the leader of this adventure — just a soldier doing her duty. We'll have pirates and Bloodseekers to deal with, but it's all in a day's work in a world where danger and wonder co-exist.

For now, I've got to get my head around the idea of a compassionate mission, looking across The Hallowed Lawn as Casper and Philomeena offer reassuring words to the fallen trio. It was Kaira's dad and aunt who looked after me in my early days, forgiving my misdeeds as I found my way.

Now, they're asking for the same level of compassion from me. As much as I trust their judgement, Thylas' final vision hovers in my mind ... high in the Devreack sky ... of a boy consumed by power and blinded by hatred.

"This part doesn't need an audience," Farraday states as the ash falls away from Alice, Mae and Fillian: a sign they've passed the loyalty test. "We'll make our way back to The Cendryll, leaving Casper and Philomeena to complete the ritual."

No one argues, happy one problem is being resolved without harm, light beams fading in the sky as Farraday creates a Cympgus for us all: a portable Perium to take us home. Conrad gestures for me to follow him through the circle of purple light, but I pause, looking back at three ex Night Rangers who were once so confident, hanging off Taeia's every word.

He might have found exile in the sky realms, but Thylas' vision tells me judgement's waiting around the corner, delivered in a storm of blows when a boy-king blasts into sight, trying to disrupt destiny. We'll be in position when he does, guided by redemption but ready for the expected *collision*.

As light drips from the bottom of the S.P.M.A. logo hanging in the sky, I whisper for Conrad to wait, halting our exit to watch Alice, Mae and Fillian lifted into the air, perched within the logo of light like birds returning to their nest.

Having survived their assessment, the final act begins, the glittering light of the S.P.M.A. logo spinning at incredible speed before it shoots off into the distance — Alice, Mae and Fillian hanging on for dear life as they dart through the sky.

"Where do you think they're headed?" Conrad asks, smiling at the sight of another act of compassion.

"To places they've never been, probably," I reply, brushing ash out of Conrad's hair. "Maybe to remind them of what they almost lost."

"The logo's a cool trick," Conrad adds as Kaira's dad and aunt make their own exit, leaving only us on the boundary of The Hallowed Lawn.

"The symbol for a place beyond dreams," I say, reaching down to touch a gathering of ash near my feet. I wonder if there's still life in the ashes, remembering the way they spun into visions of sacrifice. Either way, it feels comforting to hold the remains of old comrades in the palm of my hand, blowing them into the wind softly as a way of communicating my thanks.

"Maybe we'll rest here someday," Conrad says.

"Assuming we ever get to be legends, that is."

"You're already a legend, Guppy Grayling: the famous Fire Witch."

"Well, let's hope this Fire Witch can handle another battle."

"You can handle anything."

"I like your confidence."

"I'm blinded by love," Conrad jokes, bowing comically.

He gets the laugh he hopes for, falling backwards into our portal home as he pulls me with him. As we tumble into our glimmering Cympgus, I smile at the sight of a slide stretching ahead of us: a perfect antidote to the heavy-handed lesson delivered to our three comrades — comrades who've been given a second chance, flying through The Society Sphere on their own adventure.

Death and battle can wait for a while, giving me time to enjoy the *wonder* of magic. I'll take a morning flight with Conrad, maybe, gliding over The Winter Quarter while everything's quiet — thankful for a few moments of peace before the stars fall out of the sky, and duty calls once more.

Pre-order Book 4

TEASER CHAPTER BOOK 4

The top of The Cendryll's skylight is a comfortable place to be in the current climate, the mood of the magical faculty returning to a familiar quiet. It's been a few days since Taeia Renn gave into his darker impulses, drawn to the pirates of Kelph bursting through the skies on the back of black Williynx: a sign of things to come.

We've learned a lot since our Night Ranging duties were halted: how to fly through the skies on paths of lightning and ropes of fire, the importance of a dead Winter King's visions and the likelihood that battle is around the corner again. I'm calmer than I thought I'd be, sitting alongside my trusted crew, watching the beam of light wash over Society Square.

Sometimes, it's hard to compute how much my life has changed in the last few years — from a sullen, impulsive girl to a Society Soldier. The Society for the Preservation of Magical Artefacts is never boring, that's for sure, and it's about to get *a lot more* interesting in the next few days.

The Society elders are locked away in endless meetings, Scribberals used to transport messages to and from The Orium: the faculty where all laws and critical decisions are made.

Whatever decisions *are* made, it's bound to involve us: Jacob, Kaira, Conrad, Lucy, Noah and me. Jacob's got his teaching responsibilities but is already committed to defending the sky realms: a shimmering matrix hidden in the stars.

If Kelph is a taste of things to come, it's going to get hairy up there ... just like it did when I first stepped beyond the Society Sphere ... across mountainous ranges towards the ashes of Moralev ... before coming face-to-face with a legendary beast in the Caves of Varakel.

The difference this time is we've got enemies *and* new magical laws to master: material magic forming the principles of sorcery in the sky realms. It's less about creation than manipulation, something shown to us in glorious form when Thylas Renn drew thunder and lightning from the skies.

Thylas was another legendary Renn burdened with great gifts: the gift of blind sight offering visions of catastrophe ... a troubled heir storming towards the throne he'd abandoned with vengeance in his eyes. It's time to make plans of our own while the adults ruminate over what to do next, meaning which of them will act as guardians when we return to the sky realms.

Farraday's already made it clear that the heavier burden will fall on younger shoulders this time. We were inexperienced witches and wizards when evil raised its head last time, following the rhythms of the surrounding adults — adults who put their lives on the line to protect us at every turn, some not making it out of battle.

We know it's going to be different this time, leading the charge to the skies to find a way of drawing Taeia back from the brink of a catastrophic choice: a mercy mission that's likely to go south when we meet our fallen comrade again.

"We never learnt to read the stars," Jacob comments from a position on top of The Cendryll's skylight. "Sianna never got around to it."

"We were a bit busy keeping up with her on the way to Devreack," Noah replies.

"At least we've learnt a different way to fly," Lucy adds, giving Noah a look.

It's a familiar look linked to her annoyance at Noah's sarcasm — losing its comical power as things get more serious.

"Maybe Sianna doesn't know how to read the stars," I suggest, "or isn't willing to teach us."

"Or it's a matter of discovery," Kaira counters, my friend returning from her sabbatical above ground. "Jacob said Taeia sat up here night after night, firing out wisps of light towards the stars, getting calmer each time. It sounds to me like Taeia discovered the stars somehow, using the magic he knew to uncover the unknown."

"Good to have you back, Kaira," Jacob replies with a smile, the Society tie he grudgingly wears for teaching wrapped around his hand. "We'll need your wisdom when we head back up there, assuming you're coming that is."

Kaira nods, sitting alongside me in the regal manner shared with her parents. "I'm ready to meet some new friends," she replies with a smile, turning her attention to the skies and the mysteries hidden within them. "First, we need to find out how to read the stars. Lucy's idea of it working like a Nivrium has got me thinking — maybe my dad and aunt know more than they're letting on."

"They normally do," Jacob replies, running a hand through his long, dark hair. "I doubt they want you to return to battle, Kaira, maybe that's why Sianna kept her knowledge of the sky realms to herself."

"Maybe, but I wasn't there when Guppy and the others returned to The Royisin Heights."

"Maybe the adults are returning to secrecy again," I suggest, glancing at the penchant bracelet on my right wrist, wondering if it will guide us at all in the sky realms. Moving beyond The Society Sphere makes its powers fade, but Thylas Renn explained the relationship between our worlds: how our knowledge can be used to call the elements towards us.

It's a lot easier than it sounds and unless we learn how to read the stars soon, we'll be flying towards danger at a disadvantage.

"My dad and aunt live in a different way now," Kaira explains, sending a streak of purple light towards the sky ... The Cendryll's beam of light acting like a lighthouse, searching for the stranded on the evening streets. Stranded can mean of lot of things, particularly in view of our current problem with a boy wizard who's found his gifts — stranded between a critical choice which is drawing competing forces towards him.

"They obviously don't want me to fight again," Kaira continues, "but we're long past that now. We're battle scarred after all — all of us in some way now — and it looks like we're leading this charge into the skies, so I say we follow Taeia's lead and unlock the mysteries in the skies."

"How?" Noah asks, containing his habit of sarcastic replies.

"With magic," Kaira replies as she fires another streak of light into the evening sky: a warrior girl who's returned to the fold at a critical moment.

The rest of us join Kaira in our study of the stars, sending streaks of light upwards in the hope of discovering something or, at least, *connecting* to something but nothing happens beyond our shower of light fading like fireworks: our moment of fun fizzling out. Whatever Taeia saw or sensed up here isn't being picked up by us — Society warriors not aligned to the sky realms in the way our exiled king is.

"We could sit up here night after night, but I doubt it would tell us anything," Noah comments as we send more streaks of light into the sky ... this time making them stretch as high as possible ... like rockets reaching for the moon. "The irony of it all is that Taeia's ended up being more gifted than we are."

"Marked with different magical abilities," Jacob counters, clearly not happy with the idea of a questionable wizard being superior to us. "We'll only find out if he's more powerful when we meet him again."

"Sounds like life and death," Lucy adds, standing on the top of The Cendryll's skylight to study the glimmering sky.

"Hopefully, no one has to die," I reply. "A lot depends on how quickly we can locate Taeia's whereabouts."

"In Kelph," Noah adds, standing to join Lucy — the white T-shirt hanging over his chinos.

"A realm waiting for our return," Conrad adds alongside me, a strange quiet falling over him.

I wonder if talk of war reminds him of his dad's sacrifice — an incredible act of bravery in The Saralin Sands. Kaira lost her granddad too, maybe explaining why they've both retreated into themselves a little: as if the trauma's resurfacing. We've got more than physical scars but none of us have expressed any regret.

There's nothing like the S.P.M.A. — a place I'm planning to live and die in. I barely think of the above-ground world now: a place whose wonders have long faded from my memory. Let's face it, after you've stormed through the sky on paths of lightning, whipping out ropes of fire to increase your momentum, there's not much incentive to return above ground.

Our Night Ranging duties will resume at some point, assuming we all survive what's ahead, a time when we can return to the fun of Rebel's Rest, telling our Society friends all about our adventures in the skies. Conrad edges closer as Jacob releases a flurry of Quij: a simple trick of blowing on his hands and closing his eyes, releasing the luminous creatures.

Usually asleep once night falls, Quij can be called upon in times of need. Jacob's called them for comfort more than anything else: a brother with a strange connection to Society creatures.

I want to ask him what he saw in the mirror — the one spun into life using his Vaspyl when Taeia escaped from The Cendryll — but that's for another time. Tonight's about rediscovering old bonds and reflecting on what's passed: a meeting with a fading Winter King and a run in with the leaders of Kelph ... not to mention the Bloodseekers who lined the skies on our return to The Society Sphere ... striking in looks and deadly of spirit.

I can't say I'm looking forward to bumping into them again, although when I do I'll make sure I've got an exit strategy. The S.P.M.A. is a peaceful Society after all, so killing isn't part of the script — which isn't to say I'm going to let the Bloodseekers kill *me*. I'll just have to be creative when the time comes.

"I wonder what he saw?" Lucy asks as she keeps her gaze on the stars. "Taeia, I mean."

"Something only a Winter King is attuned to, probably," Jacob responds, holding his hand out for the Quij to rest on. "I was up here every night with Taeia and didn't see or sense anything, even when he started to change. He's found his calling and it's going to be hard to persuade him back from the path he's chosen."

"Mainly because he hates us all," Noah comments, reaching for Lucy's hand who brushes it away. Romance clearly isn't on her mind at the moment — her theory of the sky realms working like a Nivrium on hold for a moment. It makes sense that they might, their changing formation reflecting the temperature of things up there, but the fragile triangle of allegiance isn't presenting itself to us so we're none the wiser.

"Aarav and Casper mentioned the realms surrounding Devreack — Whistluss and Zordeya," Conrad adds, deciding to form a circle of tanzanite light above us. "Casper also said we'd get a call from whoever needed us once Taeia makes his mark."

"Which won't be long," I state, using the Canvia charm

to add some stars within Conrad's circle of light. "If only we could sense what Taeia did ... not being able to puts us at a disadvantage."

"The tables turned, you could say," adds Kaira as she looks down through the skylight, tracking the movements of a familiar figure moving towards The Seating Station on the ground floor.

"Meaning?" Lucy asks.

"Meaning Taeia was always at a disadvantage down here, mainly because of his limited gifts as a wizard. We now know why that was: he was destined for greatness elsewhere. The question is, how he's going to react to our arrival now the odds are in his favour?"

"It sounds like you already know, Kaira," I say, happy to have my friend back even though it feels different this time.

"I don't but I think Farraday will: the perfect person to answer the question."

"He's hardly going to welcome us with open arms," Noah comments as he adds the colours of the rainbow around the circle of light above our heads, "which makes our mercy mission a little tricky."

"Precisely," Kaira replies, "although the real question is where the mercy lies."

"With us obviously," I reply, judging from Kaira's expression it might not be that simple.

"Maybe," she says, studying Farraday who's pacing around The Seating Station.

"I say we end our star gazing and keep Farraday company," I suggest. "Looks like he's got problems of his own."

"Or the same one," Jacob counters, ushering the Quij towards him before he places them on the glass skylight, their delicate wings fluttering as their colour intensifies ... just as a string of light stretches out from their bodies and through the skylight … fine ropes of colour for us to make our descent towards a legendary warrior, pondering what lies ahead.

As we slide down towards the ground floor of The Cendryll, touching down on the logo dominating the marble floor, I make a secret wish that Farraday can be spared battle this time: the man who's given so much and is so heavily marked by battle.

Mercy is the mission, after all, and who's to say it shouldn't begin at home? To the adults who deserve it most, leaving a group of young warriors to navigate their way to the sky realms once more, on the hunt for a king in exile.

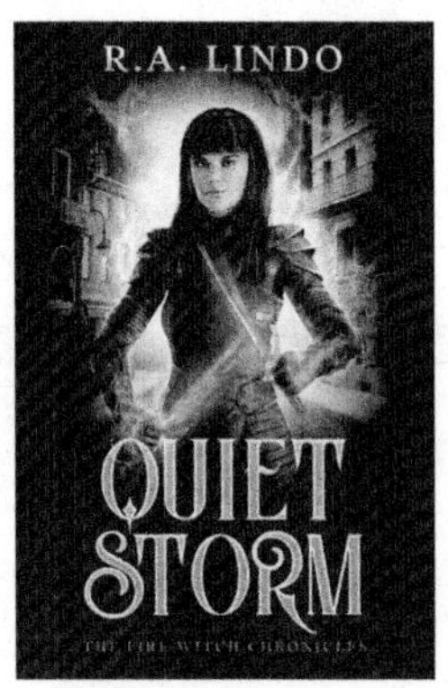

Buy Book 2

ABOUT THE AUTHOR

I'm the author of the **Kaira Renn** series, **The Fire Witch Chronicles** and **Magic & Misdemeanours**, all set in The Society for the Preservation of Magical Artefacts. (S.P.M.A.)

If you enjoyed the book, please consider **leaving a review on Amazon.**

To receive updates and a chance to win free copies of future titles, sign up to my newsletter **here**.

You can also join my **Facebook group** dedicated the S.P.M.A. universe.

ALSO BY R.A. LINDO

<u>THE S.P.M.A. UNIVERSE</u>

5 books per series

Kaira Renn Series: origin series

The Fire Witch Chronicles: spin-off series one

Magic & Misdemeanours: spin-off series two

Printed in Great Britain
by Amazon

21007377R00119